THE LAST
GARGOYLE

THE LAST GARGOYLE

PAUL DURHAM

Crown Books
for Young Readers
New York

Text copyright © 2018 by Paul Durham
Jacket art copyright © 2018 by Sebastian Skrobol

All rights reserved. Published in the United States by Crown Books for Young Readers, an imprint of Random House Children's Books, a division of Penguin Random House LLC, New York.

Crown and the colophon are registered trademarks of Penguin Random House LLC.

Visit us on the Web! rhcbooks.com

Educators and librarians, for a variety of teaching tools, visit us at RHTeachersLibrarians.com

Library of Congress Cataloging-in-Publication Data is available upon request.
ISBN 978-1-5247-0020-1 (trade) — ISBN 978-1-5247-0056-0 (lib. bdg.) — ISBN 978-1-5247-0022-5 (ebook)

Printed in the United States of America
10 9 8 7 6 5 4 3 2 1
First Edition

Random House Children's Books supports the First Amendment and celebrates the right to read.

For Wendy, the first to read every book.
And for Caterina and Charlotte,
who are still too scared to finish this one.

What is the meaning of these unclean monkeys, these strange savage lions, and monsters? To what purpose are here placed these creatures, half beast, half man, or these spotted tigers? Surely if we do not blush for such absurdities, we should at least regret what we have spent on them.

     —Saint Bernard of Clairvaux
        (twelfth century) . . . on gargoyles

1

What Goes Bump in the Night

My earliest memory is of a crib, a darkened room, and three shadows slipping through the doorway with bad intentions.

You'd be surprised how many first memories include a visit from the shadows. Parents like to stamp these visitors with convenient labels. Nightmares. Figments. Overactive imaginations.

They have other names, though. Shadow Men. Dark Wanderers. Netherkin. Names that aren't so neat and tidy.

This first memory is a very old one. Gaslit street-lamps glow outside my building. The road below is quiet, the carriages parked and the horses all stabled for the night.

The three Shadow Men flicker by the doors. The One in the Hat hovers in the middle, his eyes white slits in an otherwise featureless face. The One with the Horns stands to his left, studying the crib with a hunger I sense but cannot see.

Maybe if I lie very still they won't see me. Maybe, if I'm lucky, they won't realize I'm here at all.

It's the third shadow that steps forward first. The One with the Teeth. Gleaming, white and perfect. Odd, since nobody had perfect teeth back then.

He creeps toward me without a sound, an eager but cautious prowler.

My insides are churning. I force myself not to budge. *There's no one here,* I repeat silently to myself. *Nobody at all.* As if my thoughts might be enough to convince him.

The One with the Teeth hesitates but keeps coming. He hovers over the crib and I see his perfect mouth twist into a wicked grin. He reaches down toward the blankets, long black fingers grasping for a small foot or toe.

I allow myself to smile too.

The One with the Teeth has taken my bait.

I catch him by his wrist. He recoils in surprise but I hold fast, punching my other hand right through him. It leaves a transparent hole that I peek through, offering a wink to his sinister companions by the door. I open my fist and study the handful of smoky black essence steaming between my fingers.

It smells pungent and sour, so of course I give it a taste.

The One with the Teeth's own mouth goes wide, and he promptly collapses in a flutter of vapor.

I spring over the rails of the crib, but the One in the Hat and the One with the Horns are quick. Their forms break apart and scatter like a flock of frightened birds, disappearing into the cracks of the walls before I can do worse.

I glance back at the crib and its tiny occupant. A young boy tosses and turns fitfully in his blanket, his face hot and flushed as his lips tremble in his sleep. But he has nothing more to fear. The Shadow Men won't return on this night or any other. Not if I have anything to say about it.

Don't look so surprised—I never said the crib was *mine*.

What goes bump in the night?

If you're lucky, I do.

2

TERRIBLE CHILDREN

I'm watching you.

That's right, up here. At the edge of the roof just above the fifth-floor window. Not sure how you could miss me—I'm about the only thing of interest on this old brick building. Although, to be honest, you're not the first to walk right by.

No, I am *not* a gargoyle. I don't collect the rain and whistle it out my lips to keep your shingles dry.

Gargoyles—a bunch of glorified water fountains, if you ask me.

I am a Grotesque. One painstakingly chiseled by my

Maker nearly a hundred and thirty years ago. You may see my toothy canine jaws, watchful eyes, alert ears, and regal wings, and call me a monster or demon. That's only because you've never met a real monster before.

You can thank *me* for that, by the way. Not that I need thanks. I am here to keep you safe. I am a warden of the night. Behind this heavy stone façade lies a quick and clever protector—the most loyal friend you'll never meet. All I ask in return is that you keep the pigeons off my head.

My Grotesque friends, the Twins, say I get too riled up over those feathered menaces. But how would you feel if someone used your head as a toilet without so much as an apology? Sometimes, when I'm short on patience and no one is looking, I'll snatch one between my jaws. That usually keeps the rest of the disgusting flock away.

Yes, I can move my stone form, although it comes with a heavy price. A simple gesture like the pigeon chomp and I might need to sleep for a week. To actually get out of my crouch and run or fly, that could put me out of commission for months . . . even years. I've only had to do that once—long ago. I have no plans to do it again.

A word of advice. Should you ever see a Grotesque take to the skies by night, latch your doors and leave on the lights. It's a sure sign that serious trouble is on the prowl.

When I do move, like that time with the three Shadow Men by the crib? It's outside of my stone body in the form of a *wisp*—an apparition that exists but can't touch or be touched by the living. I'm supposed to be on my way to make just such a trip right now, but it seems I've overslept. It was an unseasonably warm autumn day, and only now, with the chilly evening air interrupting my slumber like hands tugging off a blanket, do I realize I'm late yet again.

The weather has taken an unexpectedly poor turn while I've snoozed. A strong storm is on its way in, the kind that sinks ships and punishes houses along the seacoast. I squint out toward the downtown skyscrapers and can hardly believe my eyes. Tiny white flakes and shards of sleet dance over the cityscape.

From my roof, I have a good view of the shimmering glass-and-steel tower on Boylston Street—the second-tallest building in the entire state. I see that more window panels have fallen from its highest floors, where empty frames gape like punched-out teeth. The local authorities will block the sidewalks with yellow tape while they tend to the shattered glass, and will surely chalk it up to faulty engineering or the night's gale-force winds.

But I know better.

What's obvious, at least to a trained eye like mine, is that some uninvited nuisance has taken up residence atop the tower. I was supposed to meet the Twins—Winifred and Wallace—to find out exactly what.

I can already imagine their grating voices.

Penhallow, you lazy buttress, where've you been?

Penhallow, just once can you hop your perch and be on time?

"Penhallow! Is that pigeon paint on your shoulder?"

That last one was Winnie's real voice, her tone as biting as the squeal of a streetcar braking on the tracks.

I glance down. A girl and an enormous, beady-eyed rat look up from the sidewalk.

"You were supposed to meet us an hour ago," Winnie continues. She points toward the glass tower in the distance, then thrusts both hands impatiently onto her slender hips.

"You've missed all the fun," Wallace adds. He stands upright on his hind legs, balancing himself with his ugly pink tail.

The Twins have assumed their wisp forms. Winnie favors the appearance of a forlorn girl, a waif in a ragged jacket and mesh trucker's cap over sad, lost eyes. Wallace isn't much for fashion and prefers the utility of traveling as a sewer rat. Commuters in neckties and raincoats bustle right past them without a second glance. As wisps they remain nearly invisible, and to the under-evolved ears of human passersby, our conversation is indistinguishable from the bluster of wind through the alley or the churning rumble of traffic.

"Sorry," I call down. "I overslept."

"Hold on," Winnie says. "We're coming up." She glances at Wallace. "Race you!" she declares, and darts toward the door without further warning. Wallace curses and scurries for a wall.

I'm more preoccupied with the swirling gray sky than the Twins' footrace. The ground is still too warm for snow to stick, but ice coats power lines and limbs that still stubbornly hold their red and orange leaves. With the howling wind, trees will fall tonight. Deep roots will be torn up, long-settled earth disturbed. A night for trouble.

The kind of night that could wake the dead.

Fortunately, we don't see that kind of trouble much anymore. It's a good thing, since the Twins and I are the only three true Grotesques left in this entire city. Sure, look up at the arches and eaves, especially over the libraries and cathedrals, and you'll see many carvings: heavy-browed green men, mighty chimeras, and winged griffins. But those are just fossils. Abandoned shells. They've all finished their tasks and moved on to whatever's *Next*. You can tell by the eyes. All those old friends—their eyes are now as lifeless as granite countertops.

Not mine, though. If you look at my eyes, particularly

at dusk after I've had a good day's rest, you might see a little twinkle. That's the sign of a good Grotesque—one who's always on his toes.

Wallace's own hairless rat toes appear on the edge of the roof. He pulls his chubby body up just as Winnie bursts from the stairwell.

"I win!" she calls.

"No way. It wasn't even close," Wallace objects. They hurry over to me.

"Penhallow?" Winnie asks, and they both look to me for a verdict.

"I wasn't watching," I say distractedly.

The Twins grumble. Wallace twitches his nose in annoyance.

"It's snowing," I point out.

"Just a few flakes," Wallace says.

"It's only October," I explain, and try to jog my rather long memory. Flurries this early have to be some sort of record.

"What's wrong, Penhallow?" Winnie teases. "Afraid you're going to get icicles on your tail?" She gives me a playful swat on my hard, cold rump.

"No," I say quickly. Although, indeed, there's nothing more embarrassing than an icicle hanging from your hindquarters for three weeks on end.

"Do you remember the last time it snowed this soon?"
I wonder aloud.

Wallace scratches an ear and thinks.

"Never mind all that," Winnie interrupts. "Guess what we found in the tower?"

"Oh, I don't know," I say, feigning ignorance. "Maybe . . . *imps*?"

She frowns. "Well, that was no fun. How'd you know?"

"You've still got some imp on your lip."

Winnie wipes a sticky black residue from the corner of her mouth with the back of her hand. "Thanks for telling me," she says to Wallace, shooting him a glare.

Chasing imps is a favorite pastime of ours. They are stubborn, mischievous little spirits, and once they settle in somewhere they're as persistent as bedbugs. A family of them used to live in the old brick ballpark not far from here, and it took the Twins and me the better part of a century to finally send them on their way. The good news is that imps aren't normally dangerous to people—although the recent window-breaking presents its fair share of hazards.

"Did you get them all?" I ask.

"The big ones, anyway," Winnie says. "Then Wallace got a stomachache."

Wallace places a paw on his gut.

"I've never seen so many in one place," she adds.

"I wonder what's made them so bold," I say.

Winnie shrugs. "Well, they're not going anywhere. Maybe next time—if you actually join us—you can ask them." She scowls at me, but it's more in jest than anger. "But now that you've gotten your beauty rest, we should get going. If we don't make it to the Dragon soon, we'll miss the first set."

It's Tuesday, which means live music at the Copper Dragon. Music is another favorite pastime. Sometimes it's the only thing left that inspires me to pry my heavy eyelids open on a cold night. It's another reason I'm so surprised I overslept.

"Okay," I say. "Just let me check on my wards first...."

My *wards* are the inhabitants of my *Domain*—the building on which I dwell.

Winnie groans and rolls her eyes toward the bill of her cap. "You always take *soooo* long."

"You live on an abandoned chapel," I remind her. "That's why *you're* always ready so fast."

"Maybe so, but that squatter in the basement sleeps very well thanks to us," Wallace remarks. He twirls a whisker between nubby nails.

"You go on ahead," I offer. "I'll catch up as soon as I'm done."

"You're such a stickler," Winnie says, turning on a heel. She glances back before leaving. "But you're our stickler, so we like you anyway." She gives me a wink and a tip of her cap. "Promise you won't be long?"

"Yes, I promise," I grunt.

"Good." Winnie nods, and the Twins hurry off, disappearing onto a neighboring roof.

My Domain is shaped like the letter *H,* its walls framing a small garden-entryway in the front and an even smaller courtyard around back. The unusual layout allows me to see into most of the windows without even leaving my perch—at least the ones not covered by the sprawl of overgrown leaves. My Domain is the only one on the block that wears a woolly green coat of ivy. It reminds me of the hairy man on the second floor who sometimes checks his mailbox without a shirt.

I take a quick glance down into the fourth-floor apartment, where a new family has just moved in. There are still boxes to be unpacked in the daughter's bedroom, although she ignores them and instead huddles at a brightly painted desk too small for her long legs. Her outgrown work space is a pastel blue-and-yellow island in a sea of brown cardboard. The girl labors over something—homework, or perhaps a journal—the strain on her face palpable as she puts her thoughts on paper. She has a brother still in diapers who sleeps with their mother in the bedroom across the hall. No father lives with them from what I can tell. I'll know more once they've settled in.

I cast my eyes toward the fire escapes and narrow alleyways, studying all that can be seen and, more importantly, unseen. The shadows are benign for the moment. I'll check the stairwells and basement before I leave, but it appears that my wards can spare me for a few hours.

Yes, I know, my elders would be appalled that I left my post. After all, my primary responsibility—my *only* responsibility—is to protect my Domain. But the fact is, we all stretch our wings a bit on this side of the world. This isn't the twelfth century. We aren't as uptight as those stone-faced Europeans.

The French call us *enfants terribles*. Terrible children.

To that I say, *Boucle-la, Monsieur Stone-Face.* All work and no play makes Penhallow a dull boy.

Of course, if you happen to be in Paris, please keep that to yourself.

3

THE COPPER DRAGON

I ride a green trolley as it lumbers underground. I'm just a wisp, crowded among fellow passengers who stare out into the blackness of the tunnels or the even darker holes of the electronic devices clutched like talismans in their hands. The ones closest to me frown and struggle with their phones, losing signals and dropping calls. My presence always seems to wreak havoc on the invisible signals that power these strange machines.

Don't ask me why. I'm a Grotesque, not a scientist.

The woman in front of me shivers as if something just

crawled up her neck. She glances over her shoulder but sees nothing.

No, it wasn't *me*. Remember, as a wisp I can't touch or be touched by the living.

That's not to say I flit and flutter about, or magically appear like fingers of steam from a sewer grate. In wisp form I walk, or, if I was willing to demean myself like Wallace, scurry and scamper. Except when I'm running late—like now. Then I take the subway.

If you *were* to see me as a wisp, you might mistake me for a sullen boy dressed all in black, hiding my slouched shoulders under a puffy thrift store ski vest I wear like armor. My dark eyes are always fixed on the ground, and aside from the thin white scar through one eyebrow, my face is unremarkable and mostly obscured by the hood of a charcoal sweatshirt. Maybe my skin is darker than yours, or lighter. Maybe you think I'm homeless, or up to no good. Whatever it is, if you glimpse me at all, it sets you on edge for reasons you don't entirely understand. You avert your eyes, and then, when you look back, I'm gone.

But most, like the woman in front of me who still hasn't discovered the small spider creeping across her scarf, don't even notice me at all. It's amazing how oblivious people are to what's really going on around them.

Except for the little ones, that is. The little ones can spot me without too much trouble.

A small boy stares at me from his mother's lap. He's no more than five. Instead of a tiny electronic master, in his hand he clutches a hairy blue puppet with a bulbous nose. It bears a striking resemblance to an unlucky imp I once caught in the courtyard of my Domain. The puppet, not the boy, although the kid's no cherub either.

I give the boy a slight, chipped-tooth smile from under my hood. Then I shift among the crowd of passengers and disappear.

I get off at my stop and hurry up a stairway that smells of sausage carts and restrooms. The intersection is busy with traffic and pedestrians battling umbrellas turned inside out by the storm. A street performer plucks his guitar under the archway of a small, forgotten chapel wedged between a college bookstore and a packed cafe. The upturned hat at his feet is damp and empty. I pause and look up at the Twins' Domain.

The Twins and I share a Maker—the same master stone carver created all three of us long ago. Winnie and Wallace are a chimera—goat's and lion's heads sprouted from a rodentlike body with a serpent's tail. Winnie's bearded chin and toothy mouth are open in a permanent wail, while Wallace is the more watchful of the two. His clawed paw rests on his billowing mane, shielding his eyes as he studies the horizon. Their shared body is a twisted knot of granite scales, fur, and hooves.

Clearly, I got the good looks of the bunch.

Of course, the Twins aren't home right now. Even if I didn't already know they were waiting for me at the Copper Dragon, I'd be able to tell by their cold, vacant eyes. Winnie's sure to give me an earful for lagging, but she'll get over it soon enough. With so few companions, we don't have the luxury of holding grudges.

I continue past the Twins' Domain and take a shortcut across the isolated, wooded green space called the Fens. It's quiet out here. Funny that in a city with more than half a million residents, one filled with brick and concrete and artificial lights as far as the eye can see, it's the empty spaces that make people the most ill at ease. There's little foot traffic here after dark, at least not the kind *you* can see. Fallen leaves shuffle and take flight in the community gardens before scattering in a mini cyclone. Reeds bend and sway along a muddy stream. Just the storm's influence, perhaps. But the Fens are surrounded by hospitals, and even the finest physicians lose patients from time to time.

It's not unusual for the newly dead to become disoriented out here before finding their way to a more permanent destination.

As I walk along the old stone bridge, it looks like a different kind of lost soul is heading in my direction. He's not garbed in a hospital gown. He wears shades of coal and smoke, skintight pants stretched over long legs as spindly as a vulture's. His heavy construction boots are laceless and splattered with gray clay, their tongues flapping as they clop over the stones underfoot. His dark wool sweater drapes from shoulders narrower than a wire hanger, its ill-fitting sleeves so long they cover his hands and sway against his rail-like thighs to the rhythm of his rubbery gait. The only color I see is the crimson of his scarf in the moonlight, wrapped tight around his neck and dangling like a frayed noose. A shimmering paper crown is cocked on his head and set low over his eyes, the kind the giant hamburger franchise used to give away for free with children's meals.

I pity this disheveled fellow, for clearly he is weak with illness. So weak, in fact, that it seems he's already got one foot in the grave—I can barely tell if he's dead or alive. But as I pass by unseen, I feel something else altogether. A deep gloom. Malaise. I smell the moth larvae eating the man's sweater, but he himself emits no odor or warmth. I can't help but pause for a second look, and when I glance back I'm shocked to see that he has stopped too.

That's when his head pivots to face me as if there isn't a bone in his neck, the shadows of his paper crown rendering his face featureless in the night air.

His body turns to follow his gaze, and if I didn't know better, I might think he was making his way back toward me. What he lacks in girth he makes up for with freakish height, and he walks with the odd bobble of a willow sapling dug from the earth and learning to walk on its roots. He looms even larger the closer he gets, and I'm surprised when my wisp shoulders produce an involuntary shudder. I can hear a pulse. His body may be feeble, but whatever's inside him oozes slow and thick with darkness. Is he really reaching out to touch me?

A sudden gale whips across the parkway and seems to take the man off guard, his stiltlike legs buckling from its blast. He stumbles as his ill-fitting clothes billow around him, and I watch in disbelief as he topples like an awkward scarecrow off the stone bridge and into the shallow stream below.

I hurry to the edge and peer over the side. His paper crown floats along the surface of the stream, but the clumsy wanderer himself is nowhere to be found. Lucky for him, the water here isn't deep enough to drown a rat.

Then again, my guess is that this drifter has already left the world of the living behind.

Touché, strange wobbly prince. It's not often that the dead give *me* the chills.

If I wasn't late already, I'd gladly find you and repay the favor.

There's a short line outside the Copper Dragon, where a doorman checks the ages of students who've braved the weather to wait in front of a façade of dark wood and glass. Local legend says the Copper Dragon is the oldest tavern in the city, a place where revolutionaries once plotted and schemed against their British oppressors. The former common house may be long in the tooth by New World standards, but its pedigree is just a myth made up for the tourists. A senile old specter who lived in the tavern's crawl space once told me so himself. I'm not in the habit of making small talk with the departed, but this isn't my Domain—it wasn't my job to chase him out.

I glance up at the oxidized green scales and claws of the dragon, who holds the swaying wooden placard over the door. Neither gargoyle nor Grotesque, he's as simple as a weather vane and as silent as a signpost. He's got no say in the matter either.

I can hear that the band inside is already well into its first set. The beat of an actual drum kit is accompanied not by electric guitars or the tones of synthesized keys, but by the haunting call of classical strings. Modern songs covered by real musicians playing instruments with origins as old as mine. The Twins call them music-worms. I think of them as my kind of people.

I bypass the line and slip into the side alley, climbing onto a dumpster, where I can just catch hold of the fire escape's dangling ladder. I make my way along the rungs to a landing over the door the cook keeps open to air out the kitchen. The smell of grease from the grill is particularly rancid as I approach the Twins' usual meeting spot.

"I know, I know, I'm late—" I begin to say.

But no twitching rat or brooding, impatient girl awaits me. Neither Wallace nor Winnie is here.

Instead, I find two long black streaks burned into the brick wall, like the remnants of a scorching fire. There's a lingering crackle of static in the air, but the rest of the wall and the building appear unscathed.

I reach out to examine the ominous markings but recoil at the touch. I know immediately that the scorched remains were once my friends. I sense their residue in the dark chalk of the ash, now just a simmering echo of memories.

A cymbal crashes inside the Copper Dragon and I feel an unfamiliar sensation. Alarm. My eyes dart around at the shadows. Very few things exist that could have done this. Whatever it was, it has only recently departed.

Then, just as suddenly, I am left with a dull hollow, filled only by the bass tones of a cello wafting from the tavern.

The Twins were the closest thing to family I've ever had.

Now I'm all alone, the last Grotesque in all of Boston. And I'm afraid this is just the beginning of the storm.

4

DON'T CALL ME GOYLE

My stone shell has been heavy lately. I hunker deep inside it, sleeping well past sunset. When I finally stir awake, I brighten at the prospect of evening adventures with my friends.

Then I remember. And sleep some more.

It's been several days since I discovered Wallace and Winnie outside the Copper Dragon. What was left of them, that is. Since then, I've considered venturing out to scatter some unsuspecting pigeons, or stealthily plug the mouths of the gargoyles who live in the Public Garden's fountain. But those games seem less amusing without the

Twins' encouragement. Instead, I've just spent my nights here on the roof of my Domain, my mood as gloomy as the sky.

It's not that I'm *afraid*, if that's what you're thinking. I've thought long and hard about finding whatever it was that harmed my friends, but I simply don't know where to begin. It would be helpful to have another Grotesque to talk with. Sure, there are others in places like Philadelphia and Chicago, but it wouldn't be right to leave my Domain long enough to make such a trip. The New Yorkers are a bit closer, but there's no way I'm going to ask them for help. They already look down their stony noses at the rest of us here in the New World. Never mind the fact that I'm older than most of them, or that we've always had more formidable wickedness to deal with in my neck of the woods. The Puritans' public hangings in the Common, the misguided witch trials—that sort of ugliness leaves a stain that doesn't fade quickly.

My New York neighbors will never admit it, but they have it easy—there are literally hundreds of them. With all those eyes to watch your tail, it's easy to find time to buff your claws, preen your wings atop skyscrapers, and indulge in other vanities. The only snootier bunch are the French—but at least they've earned it.

So, for the time being, I stay here rooted on my perch, as

lifeless as an August chimney. No, I'm not *procrastinating*—I'm just . . . biding my time. My Domain's a decent place to sit and think. There used to be storefronts on the first floor—a florist, a cigar shop, a busy little bodega. They flourished under my watchful eye and were never once robbed or vandalized, but they've all since been converted into apartments. My other wards—the building's residents—come and go over the years, and some are more tolerable than others.

A young Indian couple keeps to themselves, and you'd hardly know they were here except when Mrs. Pandey cooks and the aroma of Eastern spices fill the halls. There's the elderly woman who lives alone and speaks only Korean to her cats. The cats don't care for me much and have been known to bristle when I'm near. Once, the woman took a fall and lost her false teeth. After watching her gum dry toast for days, I convinced her ill-mannered pets to bat the dentures out from under the couch. The cats weren't necessarily pleased with my means of encouragement, but they wouldn't have lifted a paw to help on their own.

Several young people live together in another apartment and practice being adults. They go to one of the local universities, supposedly to acquire a variety of facts and worldly knowledge. I'm not sure how useful their learnings are; I doubt any of them could so much as lay a brick or mend a fence. Even a dripping faucet sends them clamoring for help. They often come out on the roof to celebrate occasions of dubious importance, swilling drinks from plastic cups and raising their voices so loudly they drown out their own music. Once, one of them put a red cup atop my head like a party hat.

Mortifying. It's a good thing none of the New Yorkers could see me.

Sadly, we don't get to pick our wards.

Then there's the new family on the fourth floor. They've been settling in. The girl's name is Hetty, the mother's Mamita—or that's what Hetty calls her, anyway. Hetty usually refers to her little brother as Captain Poopy-Pants or Thunder-Bottom, but I've gathered that his given name is Tomás. Turns out Hetty's father expired last summer. She's had a hard time accepting that he's moved on to what's Next. I know this because Mamita put a framed family photo of them all up in the new apartment—four joyful, smiling faces, even Captain Poopy-Pants. Hetty stared at it for a long while, then, when her mother wasn't looking, hid it away in a drawer.

It's late Friday evening and tonight Hetty has some friends sleeping over. From my perch, I can see that they've laid out colorful sleeping bags on the floor. They eat ice cream from huge bowls as they whisper and laugh. It's nice to see Hetty smile. She doesn't do it often enough.

I'm really not a busybody. Although my hearing is keener than a bat's, I only gather what I need to know in order to keep my wards safe. You've heard people say they'd like to be a fly on the wall? Take it from a Grotesque on the roof, the vast majority of conversations are terribly dull. Even if I wanted to eavesdrop on Hetty and her friends, most of their words are currently drowned out by the incessant chatter around me. A break in the drizzle has lured a few of the practice-adults out onto the rooftop again, hands thrust into the pockets of their jeans while they plot their evening adventures. They completely ignore me, as usual, which is at least better than being used as a hat rack.

When Hetty and her friends finish their dessert, her mother pokes her head in to collect their bowls and say good night. With a wink, she tells them not to stay up too late, knowing full well that staying up too late is the entire point.

After she shuts the door, the girls gather in a circle. The one with makeup around her eyes and lips, the one with bad energy that engulfs her like a winter coat, is taking out an old Ouija board from her backpack. The flat wooden slab looks aged and authentic, imprinted with the numbers 0 through 9 and the words *yes, no,* and *good bye* in an ominous black scrawl. She lays it out on the floor in the center of their little ring. Just what I need—a coven of clueless, pint-sized mediums in pajamas and slippers.

There's a shuffling of heels on the asphalt roof around me as the practice-adults make their way back inside.

Hetty and her friends place their fingers on the heart-shaped planchette and I see their lips begin to move.

That's a bad idea, Hetty. Don't open the door for them. Don't invite them inside. The dead make terrible house-guests and linger like rotten fish.

Of course, she can't hear me. And probably wouldn't listen if she could. I cringe as the planchette begins to glide along the surface of the spirit board.

Then a voice startles me.

"Hello, Goyle."

There's a girl up here. She wears knee-high leather boots, striped leggings, and a weathered pea coat. She looks several years younger than the practice-adults, but she should still be far too old to spot me for what I really am. I'm stunned that she's speaking to me.

"Please don't call me that" is the best response I can muster. "I'm *not* a gargoyle."

She frowns, sets what looks to be a black violin case on

the roof, and settles herself next to it, boots dangling over the edge.

"Sorry, you *look* like a gargoyle," she says, blinking large almond eyes at me. Loose pigtails drape over each ear from under the gray cap on her head—the kind newsboys used to wear a century ago. Her hair is inky black, except for a dyed crimson streak running through one of the pigtails.

I'm not at all comfortable with this trespasser's casual tone, and yet I feel compelled to set the record straight.

"I'm a Grotesque," I clarify.

"What's the difference?" she asks.

"The *difference?*" I repeat, aghast. "Where do I begin? Wait—you can see me? *Hear* me?"

My lips don't move like some stone puppet's—most of my "talking" takes place inside my head. Sadly, I'm usually the only one listening.

"Of course," she says, scrunching up her face. It reminds me of a cracked porcelain teacup. Shiny and smooth but sharp around the edges. To be handled with caution.

"You seem a bit old for that," I say, studying her suspiciously.

Over the years, I've come across the occasional adult or older child who can look past our shells and converse with Grotesques. The Twins and I call them *squids*. Odd creatures, every last one of them. Like squids out of water, they don't really fit in with their own kind.

They've always given me the creeps.

"What exactly do you see?" I ask.

The girl chuckles and glances up and down my stone features. "Well, you're gray and rain-worn, so I can tell you've been here for a long time. Your face is all squashed—like a pug or a bulldog. Maybe a monkey. You've got some sharp claws and your wings seem sleek and powerful, though."

Not that impressive, I think. Anyone can describe my physical form—if they bother to look.

"But what happened to your eye?" she asks, gesturing with a hand in a fingerless wool glove. Her knuckles are thick and swollen, her nails ragged and short.

She's noticed the chip in the stone above my right eyebrow. There's another in the left canine that protrudes over my upper lip, but she's nice enough not to point that flaw out.

"And your tooth?" she adds, pointing to my mouth as if she might touch it.

So much for the nice part.

"Accident," I say flatly. "A long time ago. Thanks for bringing it up."

"But that's just the outside," she continues. "Inside,

there's something dark and swirling, like a storm cloud that can't quite rain."

"Okay, I get it," I say. "You can see me." Definitely squidlike, this one.

"Should I go on?"

"No, that's quite all right," I answer quickly, trying to quell the uneasy tendrils fluttering in my gut. "How did you get up here, anyway? I didn't see you come in."

"Do you see everything?" she asks.

"Absolutely," I fib. Truth be told, I've been a bit distracted since the unsettling loss of my friends.

"The stairs," she says with a nod to the fire door. It's propped open with a cinder block. The practice-adults must have forgotten to close it again.

"You don't live here," I point out.

"No," she agrees.

"What are you, about twelve or so?" I ask, looking her over again.

She gives me a little smile. "Good guess." I see her steal a glance down toward Hetty's window.

"Do you go to school with those girls?" I ask.

She shakes her head. "I spend most of my time at the Conservatory."

The music school? I eye the old-fashioned violin case at her side with growing interest. Its wooden surface is scuffed and battered—a tiny coffin sealed with brass clasps. It's got character. I have a sudden urge to fling it open and see the instrument inside, but I mind my manners.

"Are you some sort of prodigy?" I ask.

"Something like that," she says with a shrug. "Do you like music, Goyle?"

"It depends, *Viola*," I say, intentionally misidentifying her instrument.

"This is a violin case," she corrects, patting it with a gloved palm.

"I know. And I'm a Grotesque, not a gargoyle."

She narrows an eye and purses her lips. "You're pretty clever for a block of stone, Goyle."

"You're pretty bold for a squirming lump of flesh and breakable bones, Viola," I say, and she stiffens.

Oh, bricks. That was harsher than I intended. She looks like she might leave. As strange as it is to be talking with this girl on my roof, I don't really want her to go. I haven't actually talked to *anyone* since the Twins moved on.

"Sorry," I mumble. "I wasn't implying that I would break your bones."

She glances at me warily, then down at the streetlights and a row of silent cars parked along the curb.

"So why are you up here?" I ask. "You're not hanging around with those college students downstairs, are you?

Take it from me, they're not nearly as interesting as they pretend to be, and their apartment smells like last month's laundry."

"I like it on the rooftops. If you listen closely, you can hear the songs of the city."

I could tell her that I hear the shallow breathing of the infirm at City Hospital, or the last gasps of dockworkers drowned in the great Molasses Flood long ago. But I'm afraid that might prompt her to leave again.

"Sometimes I hear things" is all I say.

Her eyes drift upward to the sky. The urban lights dull the stars here, even on the clearest night.

"We're only a few blocks from Symphony Hall," she says. "Late at night, when the streets grow still, the musicians practice. They're at it now." A small smile curls her lips. "Can you hear them?"

I have to restrain myself from jolting my stone neck in surprise. *Can* I? A string quartet is at it again. I always pause to listen—it's one of the few things that help drown out the stir of distant echoes.

She closes her eyes, tilting her neck so that her chin juts in the air, and breathes deeply.

I join her in the silence. The haunting violins carry across the rooftops like the call of invisible night birds.

Then the strings disappear in a harsh screech of static.

Sharpened nails carve at a chalkboard inside my ears. A vibration runs under the building and up its walls like a swarm of scuttling rats, until it rattles inside my body. If you've ever hit your funny bone, imagine that sensation in every limb at once.

"What is it, Goyle?" she asks, jolting her eyes open as if she senses my alarm.

I look down at Hetty's window. I see the Ouija board on the floor, Hetty and her friends huddled around it anxiously. I was afraid this would happen. Someone—*something*—has accepted their invitation for a chat.

"*Netherkin,*" I whisper sharply.

"Nether what?"

"Stay here, Viola," I say. "Don't leave the roof."

And with that I flash into a wisp and head for the basement without delay.

5

THE NETHERKIN

The only elevator in the building is a rumbling black box, one that refuses to move until you slide its heavy grating shut behind you, sealing yourself inside it like an iron coffin. It's a temperamental beast, a relic from another century, and even I don't trust it. Instead I take the narrow, deserted stairs, which grow quieter and less welcoming the deeper you descend.

The basement is a cold and windowless labyrinth, dimly lit by two exposed bulbs that flicker under thick coverings of dust. There are no apartments down here, this place only home to rattraps and a row of rusting washers and dryers. Most of my wards opt to wash their clothes at the laundromat down the street. Those who make use of the machines don't do so after dark.

Not that they have anything to fear. I keep a clean basement. No, I don't mean the cobwebs and trash overflowing from the garbage chute. What I'm fastidious about is keeping it free of unwelcome visitors of the shadowy sort. In that regard, you might call me a neatnik.

But tonight, as I creep silently through the deepest level of my Domain, I can smell the Netherkin. I know it's down here somewhere.

Don't confuse Netherkin with imps. Imps are like flies. Scavengers who were never of this world but who feed off it like parasites. Quick and numerous but weak in spirit, they can do no real harm to the living. They seldom enter my Domain, nor any other Grotesque's, for we can swallow them like candy when we catch them.

Netherkin are different. They were once part of this world and their ties to it remain strong. They exist in more forms than I can list: common haunts, malignant poltergeists, and festering specters. The sinister, shapeshifting Shadow Men are a special breed of Netherkin—the evilest of all. But what they all share is an unwillingness to move on to what's Next, for reasons both unknown and unimportant to me. What *is* important is that these vile phantoms are drawn to the living—*my* wards—and that sort of nonsense will not be tolerated in my Domain.

The only good Netherkin is a well-digested one, and I've consumed more than my fair share.

When Netherkin enter dwellings, it's most often through basements and cellars. It's no coincidence that your youngest siblings won't go downstairs to fetch that seldom-used tool kit or clean the cat's litter box alone. I told you they see things that older children and adults don't. Perhaps it's the cracks and crevices, or the proximity to the stale soil, but underground places are the Netherkin's highways of choice. Fortunately, I can feel them coming. Hear them, even—if they're particularly clumsy. The noise of tonight's unwelcome visitor is what interrupted my relaxing moment on the roof.

One of the bulbs overhead sputters and winks out. It's a sign I'm getting closer. Do you find yourself changing lightbulbs often in your home? You might want to—well, never mind.

I finally spot the Netherkin as I slip around a support beam and creep past a box of abandoned toys. In the unlikely event you should ever glimpse one with your own eyes, it may appear to you as a vague human silhouette, or an unexplained orb of light in the corner of a photograph.

Consider yourself lucky. I see them for what they really are.

This particular abomination leans over, lapping a stagnant puddle from a leaky pipe with a tongue as narrow as a serpent's. It's oddly feline, an emaciated predator without fur or skin, its body just rippling sinew and pulsing, bloodless veins. Fortunately, it's a small one, crouching on two legs like a nasty little ape, bracing itself on the pads of its long, stringy fingertips. Its pointy, batlike ears twitch alertly.

But I'm too stealthy for it. I have to cluck my own tongue in disapproval to get its attention.

The Netherkin recoils and hops around to face me. The pupils of its oversized eyes dilate into black bottomless saucers, then narrow back into slits.

"Don't let me interrupt you, Netherkin," I say. "Go on, drink your fill."

The Netherkin cowers for a moment, like a frightened animal, but doesn't move.

"So, you're finished, then?" I ask.

It huddles there without response, flexing its claws anxiously.

"It's time for you to go."

Finally, it speaks, although not with words. It's more like a vibration.

"That, I cannot," it hums.

Perhaps this Netherkin is new and stupid, and mistakes me in my wisp form for some frightened boy.

"You realize that I'm the Night Warden of this Domain?" I ask.

"I do," it warbles back.

"And you still choose to stay?"

"A choice in the matter I have none. What the Boneless King orders, must be done."

I narrow an eye under my gray hood. "That rhymes. Very cute. But you understand what happens if you ignore my demand?"

The Netherkin hesitates, tensing the muscles in its throat.

"The Boneless King's my master, iron-fisted and terse. Whatever you threaten, his wrath is worse."

I sigh at the foolish Netherkin. And they say Grotesques are stubborn as rocks.

I lower my hood. I am still a wisp, but the boyish face of my form shifts, teeth growing out of my mouth until they become sharp tusks. My skin bleeds into an ash gray, and my jacket writhes and contorts on my back, sprouting two fearsome, leathery wings. My fingers are as sharp as sickles.

I can smell the fear in the phantom, but instead of

disappearing down the floor drain or fleeing into the pipes, it rises up and postures, brandishing its jagged teeth and rotten gums.

Feisty, this one.

It springs, but I'm too fast. I step aside and it crashes off the old oil burner with a sickening thud, sending dust from the rafters. I expect the blow will have knocked some sense into it, but I'm wrong. No sooner has it regained its feet than it lashes out again.

This time I catch it with a firm grip around its throat. I pummel it against the floor like an oversized rag doll, then pitch it into the open hole of a dryer. I slam the door on its head three times, until it falls into a heap on the basement floor.

"No more warnings, Netherkin. Be gone," I command.

The Netherkin's eyes look up at me and flash. Its weakened voice is just static in the musty cellar air.

"I'm just the first but won't be the last. The Boneless King's prize shall be claimed before long has passed."

That does it. I've never had the patience for bad verse.

I dislocate my jaw and my cheeks melt like a burning plastic mask. I open my mouth until it gapes as wide as a sewer. Clutching the Netherkin by its nubby tail, I thrust him inside and swallow him whole.

The lyrically challenged Netherkin is still repeating on me as I make my way back upstairs. They always leave me with indigestion, and this one sits particularly foul in my gullet.

I reach the roof and pull on my hood, turning my attention to the evening's other visitor. But Viola is gone. It's surely for the best, and yet I find myself strangely disappointed by her absence. I listen. Sadly, the string quartet is done rehearsing too. I belch and curse the Netherkin's taste on my tongue.

I miss my friends. And now something other than the Netherkin is bubbling inside me.

Anger.

I'm tired of sitting around idly. The Twins' killer is out there and I'm not about to find him by sitting here gathering soot on the roof.

The posthumous poet in my gut may have lost his otherworldly mind, but his incessant yammering about his master has gotten me thinking. Who would dare to send a Netherkin to my Domain? I remember the limp-legged wanderer I came across in the Fens. That paper-crowned fool seemed incapable of commanding his own feet, never mind a Netherkin, and surely anyone too weak to stand up to a stiff breeze would be no threat to the Twins. But his dark thoughts pulsed with a strength beyond that of his frail body, so strongly that he just might warrant a second look.

Tomorrow I'll head out in search of this so-called Boneless King, whatever he might be. And while some glorified ghoul may not be responsible for the demise of the Twins, I'll be glad to let off some steam all over his homely undead head.

For now, I peer down into the fourth-floor window as I settle back into my stone shell on the parapet. Hetty and her friends are finally curled up in their sleeping bags. If I've done my job well, they'll sleep soundly, blissfully ignorant of all that has just transpired.

But I notice that, on this night, Hetty has left a small lamp alight atop her pastel desk.

6

DANGEROUS GROUND

Weekend traffic is light the next morning, but the buzz of visitors at the lobby call box jars me each time I nod off to sleep. A steady stream of parents arrives to collect their daughters from Hetty's apartment, until only Hetty, her mother, and Captain Poopy-Pants remain. I'm glad to see the mini-mystic with the eyeliner take her spirit board with her. There'll be no more misdirected invitations to the netherworld under my watch.

It's almost noon when I finally abandon hope of getting any rest. I rise and stretch around the same time as the practice-adults and, as a wisp, make my way down to the rear courtyard of my Domain. Surrounded on three sides by the building's walls and five stories of looming windows, the square is a constantly shifting realm of shadows. Only ivy and weeds grow here, but that hasn't stopped the building manager from placing a couple of stone benches around the tiny concrete lawn. A six-foot-high, ivy-covered garden wall separates the courtyard from the back alley. It's topped with a layer of mortar embedded with shards of broken bottles to deter unwanted visitors from climbing over. Not that it's needed. Anything a little glass can do, I can do better.

I pass cheerful old Miss Ada. She's stooped at the waist, wearing canvas sneakers and a sweater flung over her floral dress. She diligently collects litter from under the benches—undoubtedly left by the practice-adults the night before. I like Miss Ada, and even though she can't hear me I greet her with a "Hello" as I pass. Her round face squints up from her toils as if she feels a sudden breeze. Miss Ada's originally from an island in the Caribbean, but she's lived in my Domain so long she can sense the slightest change in the air. She'd make a good Night Warden.

I exit up and over the garden wall with barely a rustle of ivy—a few broken bottles don't bother me. It feels good to get out again. Today I'm making my way to a place known to be popular with Netherkin. I intend to use my special breed of charm to persuade one to tell me more about this Boneless King. I still doubt he is any sort of royalty—boneless or otherwise—but the prospect of a hunt has made me feel useful again. If I really catch a break, I may even find out who or what attacked the Twins. The thought makes me tremble with rage; then I crack a chip-toothed smile.

It's going to be a bad day for the dead.

All is quiet in the back alley, as expected. It's strange enough for *me* to be roaming under the gray midday sky; it would be extremely unusual—and problematic—to find Netherkin out by the light of day. I turn the corner onto the more highly trafficked avenue and stop short.

Hetty and Mamita have left the building too. Hetty pushes her little brother in a stroller, making race car noises as she zips him around cracks and craters in the sidewalk.

I follow them down the block. *No,* I'm not a stalker—I happen to be heading in that direction myself. But when they stop and unlatch a chain link gate, I can't help but veer off my path.

Unknowingly, my wards have just entered dangerous ground.

Colorful gnomes in puffy coats and striped wool hats dangle upside down from monkey bars. Their parents and babysitters chat and read magazines next to parked strollers, confident that the short fences will keep the little wanderers safe from the traffic creeping around their urban oasis.

Playgrounds. They're overrated. And dangerous, if you ask me.

This one has been here for decades. I can't tell you how many of my littlest wards have been sent home in need of ice packs and Band-Aids, all thanks to its cold metal hands.

Hetty and Captain Poopy-Pants are the first children to inhabit my Domain in quite some time, so I've delayed my hunt to observe them in their natural habitat—and to make sure neither of them ends up with stitches. Tomás sits in a sandbox not far from Mamita, scooping its damp dunes with an empty Play-Doh canister. I crinkle my nose. If only they knew what the local alley cats did in that box.

Hetty sits alone on one end of a bright blue seesaw. Her knees practically touch her chin and the seat of her jeans rests just inches from the leaf-strewn ground. She's by far the oldest child here. Her fingers busily fumble with something in her lap as the younger children squeal and dart past, playing a game of tag. She brushes her dark curls off her face and offers them a small, sad smile.

There's no lonelier place than a seesaw without someone to join you. I know how she feels. I'm just a wisp on a bench at the playground's fringes.

I sigh and pull my hood tighter around my face, then approach Hetty carefully. The younger children, who may or may not see me, are far too busy to pay me any mind. Hetty's eyes remain lowered. She's pulling and stretching a small handful of her brother's Play-Doh into a shape I can't make out. I wish I could climb up and join her on the seesaw, but my better judgment prevails. Instead, I just rest my palm on the empty seat.

I'm surprised by an unpleasant tingle—like a small electric shock. I pull my hand away but the sensation lingers, all around me now.

"Bunny rabbit!" a tiny voice cries out.

My eyes follow the source and I see one of the children pointing to the leaves of an ugly shrub growing along the fence. Like a swarm of moths, the rest of the children head in that direction, followed by Mamita and a few curious parents.

For heaven's sake, don't touch it. I haven't seen a rabbit in the city in recent memory. It's probably a rabid squirrel.

I turn back to Hetty and find that she has now looked up too. But instead of watching the wildlife, she seems to be staring at *me*. Or through me, more likely. She blinks her dark eyes, then pushes herself up, setting her white molding clay down on the seat before heading off in the direction of the younger children.

I'm inclined to follow but first take a quick glance at her creation. After all, I'm a bit of an expert when it comes to fine sculpture. But my eyes narrow and linger on what she's left behind on the seesaw. Why would she make *that*?

The clay's been molded into the general shape of a long, gangly man. His face is featureless, but Hetty has topped his head with a foil hat made from a gum wrapper. It's bent into the shape of a tiny crown.

I lean in for a closer look.

A rubbery, boneless . . . *king*?

I'm jolted by a harsh cry.

"Tomás!"

The words are shrill. Panicked. They come from Mamita.

Tomás has climbed out of the sandbox, but instead of chasing rodents through the bushes, he's toddled across the grounds on uneasy legs and is heading for—*Who opened that gate?*

The ominous black gate is flung wide like a hungry mouth.

I'm after him in a flash. Mamita's even faster, streaking past me. Don't believe all those statistics about cheetahs—protective mothers are the fastest creatures on this earth or any other.

But in this case, we're both too late.

Tomás clears the gate and bobbles out onto the sidewalk, just one step from the busy street and rushing traffic.

His sneaker clears the curb. There's a blaring horn. A screech of rubber.

To my relief, there's no thud of impact. A passerby steps in front of Tomás at the last moment. It's an older child who has blocked his path.

She crouches on one knee, leans in, and seems to whisper something in his ear. Tomás pivots on his heels. Blinking wildly in confusion, he rushes back inside the safety of the fence and stumbles into the arms of his racing mother. Hetty is right behind them.

The good Samaritan pushes herself up from her knee and adjusts her wool cap. Hetty and Mamita are too shaken to either notice or thank her. I know how *that* feels. A rescuer's work is often thankless.

I hurry past my jittery wards to meet her.

"Viola?"

"Voilà," she says with a theatrical bow and a flourish of her fingerless gloves.

Viola smiles broadly from under the brim of her newsboy cap. She still wears her pea coat and carries the battered violin case in her hands.

"What are *you* doing here?" I ask.

"Sorry," she says, and her shoulders slump.

My tone was more accusatory than intended. I don't have much practice with this sort of thing.

"I mean, are you coming from rehearsal or something?" I try.

She nods and shrugs. The other pedestrians continue right on by, oblivious to the tragedy that was just so narrowly avoided.

"Well, I guess I'm glad you showed up," I say. "You kept Captain Poopy—I mean, Tomás—from getting flattened by a bus."

"Someone had to do it," she says with another shrug, the instrument case bouncing in her hand.

"I was right behind him," I clarify quickly, stealing a glance back into the playground. Someone has wisely relatched the gate. Mamita and Hetty are packing up the stroller, still trying to compose themselves.

"But I suppose it never hurts to have an extra set of eyes," I add.

"You're welcome, then," Viola says.

I turn back to her.

"So you can still see me?" I ask suspiciously.

"*Yes*. Well ... barely, under that hood. You look like you're on your way to knock off a convenience store." She narrows her eyes. "You're not, are you?"

"Of course not," I scoff. "What happened to you last night? I told you to stay on the roof."

"You didn't seem all that thrilled to find me there to begin with," Viola points out. "Now it sounds like you're disappointed I left." She purses her lips and studies me curiously. "You're a funny gargoyle."

"*Grotesque*," I correct gruffly. "It's just that—it could have been dangerous."

"Because of that Netherkin business?" she asks.

"That's right," I say. "You can never be too cautious with them."

"So what *is* a Netherkin, anyway?"

I bristle at the thought of them. "Only the vilest, most noxious vermin to crawl the earth."

Viola shakes her head slowly. "Yeah ... that doesn't really help."

I sigh. Where to begin?

"Look, I'm on my way somewhere," I say, noticing the people hustling past us on the street. "I don't have time to explain right now, but thanks again for, you know, the Tomás thing."

I start to go.

"Where?" she asks.

I pause. "Out. To find somebody." My eyes flick toward the playground, where Hetty's crowned clay figure sits ominously on the seesaw.

"Are they missing?"

"No, not *find* like that. I don't know who he—or it—actually is."

"Oh, like a scavenger hunt for people," she says cheerfully. "That sounds like fun."

I purse my lips. "It's something to pass the time, anyway," I say. "And I should really get on with it."

"Can I come?"

I almost choke in reply. "With *me*?"

"Would that be so bad?" she asks, raising an eyebrow.

It sure seems like a bad idea. "Uh, I don't know," I say.

She frowns at my response but remains undeterred.

"Come on, I can help," she says. "I'll be your extra set of eyes." She bats them widely at me to demonstrate. "To help you find your missing person."

"I mean, *maybe* it won't be awful," I say reluctantly, and sigh to convey what a painful chore it will be. I don't let on that, in truth, some company wouldn't hurt right now.

"Great," she says, brightening. "You can tell me all about the Netherkin on the way."

I take that back. Small talk *is* painful.

"Let's get going," I urge. "People will think you're crazy if you stand here talking to yourself much longer."

A city dweller can pass hundreds of people in a day without uttering a single greeting to another living soul. My wards are the same way. They practically live on top of one another but do their best to avoid eye contact in the hallway. It wasn't always that way. It used to be that everyone in the neighborhood knew everybody else. But today, despite my warning to Viola, nobody gives a second glance to the girl with the violin case who mutters to herself while marching down the street. In fact, most of those we pass prefer to carry on their own conversations through the little wires dangling from their ears.

We make a quick check of the Fens but, no surprise, there's no sign of the Boneless King or any Netherkin under the stone bridge or elsewhere. I set off for a more fertile hunting ground.

"So Netherkin are basically ghosts?" Viola asks as we cross an intersection.

Her question is a tricky one. I'm doing my best to indulge her, but describing Netherkin in human words is like painting a portrait without a brush. I've never had to explain any of this before.

"No," I answer. "At least, not like the kind you're thinking of. Ghosts are in transition—finding their way from one place to another. Some do it quickly. Others get lost along the way. Netherkin are what become of the dead who *choose* to stay."

"Stay where?"

"Here. Before moving on to what's Next."

"What's *next*?" she repeats.

"That's right."

"No, I'm *asking*—what's next?"

I shrug. "Beats me. Whatever happens to you people after you die."

Viola stops when we reach the curb and furrows her porcelain brow at me. "You don't know?" she asks.

I pause to face her. "How would I? I've never been."

I think about the Twins. And the dozens of Grotesque friends who've moved on before them. Whatever's Next for us, none of them have ever come back to tell me about it.

"But you seem to play an important role in all of it," Viola says. "Guarding against ghosts . . . or Netherkin or . . . whatever. I assumed you knew how all this works."

I stand a little taller at the sound of her compliment. Why, yes, I am an important part of —wait a minute. Is she calling me clueless?

"Well, I do have my own suspicions," I add defensively. "But I doubt they're more accurate than anyone else's. Why? Do you know what comes Next?"

Viola bites her lip in thought, running her thumb and forefinger along the crimson streak in her pigtail. "I know what people have told me. Some of them are a bit more insistent about it than others. But I don't know anyone who's ever been there either." She casts a glance toward the passersby who navigate around us on the sidewalk. "And, somehow, I think whatever's waiting will be entirely . . . unexpected."

I have plenty of my own questions for this peculiar girl with the curiosity about dead things, but this hardly seems the time or place. People with such interests often find what they're looking for prematurely. If Viola sticks around long enough, maybe I'll get around to asking those questions.

"Well, whatever's Next, no good comes from putting it off," I say. "Netherkin upset the natural balance of things . . . and my wards. I've got no patience for that sort of monkey business in my Domain."

I gesture for her to follow me. Our destination isn't far. She's quiet for much of the rest of our walk.

"Goyle," Viola finally says. "Why would the Netherkin stay here? What makes them linger?"

"Rotten in life, rotten in death, I suppose." I wave a dismissive hand. "I've stopped trying to figure them out. Their brains are long since worm-eaten."

Viola frowns.

"Whatever their reasons, the only good Netherkin is a well-digested one. Have I mentioned that already?"

Viola shakes her head.

"Keep it in mind. It could save you a lot of trouble." I stop and cross my arms when we reach a corner at the edge of the Common. "But you seem to have a knack for chatting with things you aren't supposed to. If you're really that curious about what the Netherkin are thinking, maybe you can ask one yourself."

Viola narrows an eye. "What's that supposed to mean?"

I point to a drab, boxlike building sitting just outside an old burial ground like a crypt. From beneath my hood, I flash a little grin that reveals my chipped tooth.

"Come on, I'm about to introduce you."

7

THE BLACK RABBIT

The Boylston Street subway station isn't an actual crypt, but its tunnels are indeed a tomb of sorts—the last resting place of ten souls who died in a gas explosion in 1897.

We descend the dingy tile steps with a few commuters, and before we reach the inbound platform I ask Viola if she has money for the fare. I don't need any, of course, but I'd hate to get her arrested for fare-jumping. Viola waves me off and expertly ducks under the turnstile when no one else is looking.

The platform is unusually narrow. Carcasses of hulking antique trolleys, long out of service, are displayed in an enormous iron cage alongside the tracks. It's always eerily quiet here, except when a subway car rolls in, like now, announcing its arrival with a shrieking squeal as it navigates a sharp right turn.

The car's green doors slide open, but we don't get on. Instead, we wait for all the passengers to board and disembark, leaving us temporarily alone as its wheels screech and it rumbles away, disappearing into the darkness.

"Now," I say, and leap down onto the tracks. Viola hesitates.

"It's okay," I reassure her. "Just don't touch that rail right *there*." I gesture toward the one that's alive with enough electricity to incinerate her.

She carefully climbs down onto the gravel and joins me. I coax her to follow me into the dark tunnel where the trolley has disappeared.

"Down *there*?" she says in disbelief.

"You're the one who wanted to come," I remind her, but I can appreciate her hesitation. "Look, you don't need to worry. You're with me. As long as you stick close, the Netherkin won't bother you."

I don't think she's entirely convinced, but she seems to trust me enough to follow anyway.

I lead her down a narrow corridor that runs alongside the track, slipping from one cobwebbed nook to the next.

Utility bulbs are strung overhead to light the way for subway workers, although they do little except cast monstrous, spidery shadows across the ground. We step over loose mortar and puddles. A decomposing leather belt does its best snake impression and startles us momentarily.

Yes, I admit it—even I get skittish around those slithery things.

We creep around a bend where the tunnel narrows even further. I pause and take note of some graffiti sprayed on the tunnel wall. It's no masterpiece, but the features are striking—and becoming all too familiar. The crude white stick figure looms, its face blank except for hollow black eyes. On its head? The sharp points of a crown. Boneless King . . . it seems you've been getting around.

"Eww, Goyle," Viola groans behind me. She pinches her nose. "Was that you?"

"*No,*" I say quickly. "It's just a sewage leak. Now shush, or they'll hear us coming."

I lead Viola past the unpleasant portrait. I raise a finger and signal for her to stop, then ready myself.

"They should be right about . . . here!"

With a growl, I pounce around the corner, arms raised and my most fearsome grimace plastered across my face. I always love the look in Netherkin's beady little eyes when I catch them by surprise. But this time, I'm the one caught off guard. My shoulders slump. There's nothing here.

"Are you okay?" Viola asks, coming up behind me.

"Fine," I grumble.

"The way you jumped, I thought you stepped on a mouse or something."

"I was going to scare some Netherkin for you. But there aren't any here," I mumble in disbelief. I wander around our tight surroundings, examining the walls, kicking over a large rock that has settled on the tracks. "There's *always* at least one or two around."

"Maybe they stepped out for lunch?" Viola offers unhelpfully.

This is strange indeed. The subway Netherkin are usually anchored to this tunnel like barnacles. They've dwelled here for as long as I can remember. I find myself wandering farther down the track.

"Goyle, maybe we should be heading back?" I hear Viola saying behind me.

But I'm hardly listening. I'm pushing forward with purpose, peering through the shadows. They must be here somewhere. Overhead, a utility bulb flickers.

"Goyle!" Viola says, catching up to me with a scuffle of her boots. "You told me to stay close."

We both stop short at a fork in the tunnel, where the

branching track is now shrouded in darkness. The string of overhead lights has gone black. Something stares at us from the gloom.

The eyes are red—the kind you might find on a frightened albino lab rabbit.

Viola leans forward. "Is that . . . ?" she whispers, and pauses.

These eyes aren't frightened. And the rabbit they belong to stands on hind legs as long as a human's. He's hunched over, like an old man suffering from a crippling disease, and his patchy black fur is slick with oil and grease. The wretched thing looks like he's been run over by a train, chewed up, and spit back out. One of his long ears twitches as he listens to us; the cartilage in the other ear is broken, leaving it dangling over his face like a snapped tree branch.

But I have no pity for this creature. He flashes a nasty grin, and a jagged row of oversized human teeth present themselves to me.

I don't hesitate, and rush toward him. This Netherkin is as quick as a hare in a meadow, and he darts deeper into the tunnel.

"Goyle!" I hear Viola shout. "Wait for me!"

But I don't stop. I'm on the hunt now. I've never seen a Netherkin quite like this one. I hear the pad of his claws as he hurries over gravel, the sickly wheeze of his breath choking out a malevolent chuckle.

My pursuit takes me deeper into the subway than I've ever ventured before. The Black Rabbit is quick, but I keep pace. I can hear his breathing begin to labor; I can now sense his fear as he scrambles for an escape. Hop all you want, Netherkin. You can't outrun me forever.

I'm closing in. I smell mildew and wet fur as the Black Rabbit turns a corner into an alcove up ahead. I rush in right behind him and find his back pressed against a wall just steps away. We've reached a dead end. The Black Rabbit's red eyes flicker, not nearly as defiant as they were a moment ago.

"Not so smiley now, are you?" I say. "Answer my questions and I'll make this as painless as possible."

I lower my hood and crack my knuckles. The Black Rabbit raises his long, fingerlike claws to defend himself. But my victory is interrupted by a piercing sound. The Netherkin hears it too.

The shriek of wheels on metal. A trolley is distant but closing fast.

I look over my shoulder but don't see Viola. Of course I don't. In my haste, I left her alone on the tracks.

"Oh, bricks."

I glance back at the Black Rabbit. His scarred nose

twitches, bloodshot eyes watching for my next move. Surely, if I leave him, he'll disappear into the tunnels for good. But if I stay . . .

"Goyle!" I hear Viola cry out in alarm.

I grit my teeth. I really have no choice at all.

I turn and rush from the alcove, back into the tunnel and toward the main track. I spot her on the rails, the headlights of the oncoming subway car illuminating her like spotlights.

"Viola!" I call. "Viola? Can you hear me?"

But I arrive a moment too late. The green trolley roars forward. I step aside just before it fills the tunnel with its massive frame. The tight space is alive with rattling metal and flashing light. I see the expressionless faces and dead eyes of the passengers as the windows rush past me.

I pinch my own eyes tight. Oh, no, what have I done?

When I reopen them, the trolley is gone and the tunnel is empty. Reluctantly, I squint down at the tracks, but Viola's not there either. I hear heavy breathing from the darkness at my side.

Viola is pressed into a small nook, her eyes wide and her hands clutching the violin case to her chest like a shield. I don't know how the trolley missed her, but I'm grateful that it did.

"Viola," I gasp in relief, but she doesn't reply. She steps

from the nook, brushes tunnel dust from her coat, and stumbles silently down the track.

Of course, the Black Rabbit is long gone when I recheck the alcove. I think Viola's shock has worn off by the time I trudge back and join her on the inbound platform. She sits on a bench, blinking at the oversized theater billboard sealed behind smudged Plexiglas. The tortured mask of the Phantom of the Opera returns her stare.

"Viola," I say tentatively. "Can you talk?" Even if she can, I wonder if she'll ever speak to me again.

She turns to me and narrows an eye. "I was frightened," she says slowly.

I try to reassure her. "A lot of people get frightened. No need to be embarrassed about it."

"Embarrassed?" she repeats hotly. "I'm angry!"

"Angry?" I ask.

Her porcelain face is sharp as she jumps to her feet. "You left me there."

Oh, that. "I may have gotten a bit carried away ... ," I offer.

"It's not nice to abandon someone like that," Viola reprimands. She makes a fair point, but I'm not sure how I'm supposed to reply. After a moment, she just shakes her head and stares at the dirty tile floor, simmering.

"Did you at least catch your precious Netherkin?" she finally mutters.

"Almost," I say. "I had him cornered but—"

"What?" she interrupts. "You left me to be squashed and still let him get away?"

I frown. "Well, actually, what happened was—"

"Oh, never mind all that," she says, waving away my explanation. "Is that who you were looking for? That Black Rabbit creature?"

"No. I mean, maybe. I'm not exactly sure."

I purse my lips. *Maybe* it's just a coincidence that the children happened to spot a rabbit in the playground today. And *maybe* it's just a coincidence that Hetty's sculpture and the crude portrait in the subway bear an uncanny resemblance to the wobbly man I encountered in the Fens. But I tend to believe that most coincidences are actually connections that have gone overlooked.

"This is some scavenger hunt you're on, Goyle," Viola says in response to my silence, rolling her eyes toward the subway ceiling. It reminds me of the expression Winnie used to give me. "It's pretty hard for me to help if I don't know what you're looking for," she adds.

"I'm looking for someone—or something—called the

Boneless King, okay? I'd hoped some Netherkin might direct me to him."

Viola's eyes flick back at me quickly. *"Boneless King?"*

"I know, it sounds pretty ridiculous, right? But I just happened to run into someone who fit that description the other night. I didn't think much of it then—when I left him he was all . . . wet. He looked a lot like that graffiti someone sprayed on the tunnel wall, though."

I don't mention Hetty's clay sculpture left behind on the seesaw. It's the most puzzling part of all this, and some things are better kept between a Grotesque and his wards.

Viola adjusts the brim of her cap lower over her eyes. "So if there are no Netherkin down here to point you in the right direction, how will you find him?"

I've already considered that myself.

"There are some other places to fish for Netherkin," I say. "I'll check there tonight. It's best to visit them after dark."

Viola hesitates before speaking. When she does, I'm surprised by her words. "I'll come too."

"Oh," I say, furrowing my brow. I wasn't extending an invitation. "I'm, well, used to working alone."

"I don't mind joining you."

I raise the eyebrow with the thin white scar through

it. "Even after the trolley, and the abandoning, and the near-squashing?"

"I'll get over it," Viola says flatly.

I consider her offer. "I'll be out late," I mention. "I don't imagine your parents will appreciate it."

"I can pretty much come and go as I please."

Again, I hesitate. "I suppose . . . if you really want to."

"That's what friends do, Goyle," she says, measuring her words. "They stick together."

I'm not sure what to say. Viola is quiet, as if waiting for a response.

"Don't you *have* any friends, Goyle?" she asks after a moment.

I cross my arms, and my eyes wander over her shoulder to the theater billboard. On second glance, the Phantom's mask strikes me as more sad than menacing. I try to dull the pang in my stomach and push the Twins from my mind. "I used to. They've all moved on."

Viola's voice softens. "You're all alone?"

"It seems so."

"I'm sorry to hear that."

"It happens," I mutter, and glance back, dismissing her somber look with a shrug. "Friends come, friends go. They can't stick around forever."

Her eyes wander over the shadows of my face, probing. It makes me uncomfortable. I break off my gaze.

"I'll be your friend," she says quietly.

I should probably say *Thanks.* Or *I'll be your friend too.*

Instead, I say, "That's nice." Which is apparently the wrong response.

Viola just blinks and her face tightens. She doesn't say anything else for a long time.

8

FRIGHTSEERS

The looming gates of the Granary Burying Ground are locked after sunset, but tonight an ashen-faced ghoul in a torn Victorian tea dress creeps through the rows of gray headstones. Lizzy Prudence's eyes are dark and dead, in contrast with her bloodred lips, which glow in the light of her lantern. Her breath fogs the night air as she rants in a throaty crone's voice.

"Here lies the restless soul of James Otis. He foresaw his own death—struck down by lightning. Do you smell burning flesh? Look to the shadows." She waggles her blackened fingernails. "Mr. Otis has been known to wander these grounds after dark—his ears still smoking."

A dozen tourists whisper among themselves. One raises his hand to ask the ghoul a question.

Lizzy Prudence is not a Netherkin. She's not even dead. She's a guide for one of the haunted sightseeing tours that operate around the city. This time of year, business is as brisk as the rapidly changing weather. It's cold and raw. Another unseasonable snow squall may be on its way.

The sightseers stroll past slate markers that have been worn into brittle wafers by centuries of harsh winters. The graveyard flashes with light as photographs are snapped in front of the burial monuments of Paul Revere, John Hancock, and other historic figures. Those hoping to find telltale orbs or vague apparitions in their images will be disappointed—the famous people all moved on long ago.

Contrary to popular belief, cemeteries aren't exactly teeming with spooks. By the time bodies are actually laid to rest, there's been plenty of time for their former inhabitants to begin their journey on to what's Next. If you really want to be creeped out, try wandering the halls of a hospital late at night—those places are thick with the newly dead.

But the really old cemeteries, like this one, are always home to a few stubborn Netherkin. Colonial-era physicians weren't nearly as thorough as their modern descendants, and it wasn't unheard of for some unlucky patient to be buried a bit ... *prematurely*. A few of those lie here. They're some of the oldest Netherkin in the city— the type of busybodies most likely to know who's been coming and going. The kind who might be able to shed some light on the whereabouts of the so-called Boneless King.

That's why I'm focused on the ignored graves at the cemetery's fringes. The ones pressed up against the back walls of the taller, more modern buildings. Once haphazard resting places of lesser-known citizens, these are the ones that have been disturbed and rearranged neatly over the years, making way for tourist-friendly footpaths and easing the burden of modern landscapers and their mowers. These uprooted tombs are where the most restless souls tend to linger.

"Do you see anything?" Viola whispers. She huddles at the back of the crowd nearest to me. Far enough from the tourists so that no one pays her much mind, but still close enough so that it seems like she's one of them.

"No," I say, perplexed.

"Is that normal?" she asks.

I shake my hooded head. "There are *always* a few

Netherkin here. Some of them have haunted this burial ground for three hundred years."

I scan the grounds. The well-tended grass remains still.

"Why are we taking a ghost tour, again?" Viola whispers skeptically. "Do you really need an actress in bad makeup to show you where the Netherkin are?"

Lizzy Prudence is talking about the old hanging tree that once grew on the Common. She tugs the wool scarf of a bemused tourist with mock menace.

"Of course not," I say with a frown. "But it beats walking. Come on, let's mingle before we miss the bus."

After a few more photographs, the tourists file onto the double-decker bus parked on the street just outside the gates. It's painted solid black with an elaborate pattern of stylized cobwebs that spell out WICKED BOSTON HAUNTED TOURS.

Viola and I slip on unnoticed. Viola's the only child, and each of the tourists must assume she belongs to someone else. We take two seats in the very last row. Viola taps her fingers nervously on the wood of the violin case nestled in her lap.

"Why did you bring that, again?" I ask.

She runs her thumb over a scratch along its surface. "I never let it out of my sight."

"Is it valuable?"

"Priceless," she says, and gently rests both arms over the case.

The bus pulls away from the curb as we head for our next destination. Lizzy cackles over a microphone and embellishes some ghost stories as she navigates through traffic.

"Viola," I say, "you can see and talk to me."

"Well, obviously, Goyle. Unless I'm just a figment of your imagination. Do Grotesques have imaginations?"

"And you saw the Netherkin in the subway. The Black Rabbit?" I ask, ignoring her question.

"Yes," she says with a disgusted grimace. "Don't remind me."

I nod in thought. "Have you seen other Netherkin?"

"You mean today?" she replies. "I don't think so."

I shake my head. "No, I mean before. Have you always been able to see them? Speak with them?"

Viola furrows her brow. "No. Not always."

I consider this carefully. The ability to see the dead fades with age. It's not normally an acquired curse.

"So when did you first start—"

I'm interrupted by what sounds like a theatrical organ from a haunted theme park. It's the horn of the bus. Lizzy Prudence honks as we roll past a crowded tavern, where creatures of the night in flannel shirts and white baseball caps hoist cups at curbside tables and howl at the moon in reply.

That's when I finally feel it. The crawl of energy like insects up my spine. No, it's not the baying of the tavern patrons. It's a different feeling—one that should have visited me at the Granary.

Netherkin.

I slide across the seat and press my face to the window. I look past the blur of headlights. I filter out the noise of street-side conversations and endless footsteps on pavement.

There, in the alleyway, two red eyes stare back out at us. And they don't belong to just any old Netherkin.

I'd bet my left wing those are the eyes of a Black Rabbit.

The bus inches along and the eyes blink away. When we stop at a traffic light, they reappear in a darkened doorframe.

I let out a low grumble.

"What is it, Goyle?" Viola asks.

I raise my scarred eyebrow and reply under my breath. "It seems we have company after all."

We all climb off the bus at the next stop and follow a red-brick path along the sidewalk. It leads up a hilly North End street overlooking the city's most famous Revolutionary-era church. We're met by an unexpected welcome party. A stampede of rats scurries past us in the opposite direction. I hear a startled screech of tourists, followed by laughter.

"Gross," one of them drawls. "Where are they all going?"

I watch the parade of long pink tails disappear behind us and offer a moment of silence in memory of my friend Wallace.

It's not where the rats are headed that interests me. The real question is what they're running from.

I don't have to wonder for long. Immediately I feel a difference in the air when we arrive at Copp's Hill Burying Ground. Viola hovers near the gate without entering while the rest of the tourists slowly file up the granite steps behind Lizzy Prudence. Viola grips the wrought-iron fence as if to steady herself.

"Are you coming?" I ask, looking over my shoulder at her.

"Yes," she says hesitantly. "I just feel a bit ... light-headed all of a sudden."

She hurries to follow before I can caution otherwise.

Copp's Hill is the second-oldest burying ground in

the city, but this one isn't home to dignitaries or famous patriots. The grounds are littered with the bones of the working class. Headstones memorialize artisans and merchants, while hundreds of others lie in unmarked graves. Brick buildings and narrow, uneven streets line the plot on all sides.

The tourists seem to sense the difference here too, even if they can't put a finger on what it might be. Their playful banter has been replaced with nervous whispers. Couples lock arms and hover close to Lizzy—as if the costumed chaperone can actually protect them from what inhabits the dark.

Fortunately, none of them can see what I see, otherwise they might stampede out the gate like the rats.

Over the burial ground, the night sky tumbles in shades of crimson and purple. It's the color of a violent, bruised sunset—even though twilight was hours ago. The low canopy of clouds is alive with an ominous energy that smothers the city lights.

Viola joins me as I try to focus on one of the rolling patterns overhead.

"Something's not right," she says, her voice flat and far away.

"You don't know the half of it," I grunt.

I study the mass of energy as it twists and coils. What

seemed haphazard at first glance now takes a loose shape. Black and blue fingers curl in on themselves like a divine fist beckoning—although I'm quite certain this hand has not reached down from the heavens. My eyes struggle to trace what would be a wrist and forearm, then a crooked elbow and biceps. After a moment I am able to make out its source. On the far side of the cemetery, just outside its spiked iron fence, a row of closely packed brick buildings glow as if on fire. But they're not burning.

The sickly, emaciated arm of vapor reaches up from the buildings and across the burial ground, like an enormous corpse grasping from a grave. But I can see it pulse with life, growing thicker and stronger with each passing moment as it draws in the dark, swirling energy like a magnet.

Lizzy Prudence has directed the tour group toward an ornate memorial not far from the cemetery entrance. She begins telling the story of witch trials and a crazed old minister who oversaw them. But I'm not interested in a history lesson. My eyes are on the field of headstones spread out over the hill. Darting through them, hurrying for the block of glowing buildings on its hind legs, is a dark silhouette.

A hideous, oversized rabbit.

He won't get away again, but this time I remember not

to abandon Viola. Her silent treatment after our trip to the subway was more biting than a Netherkin's teeth.

"Viola, follow—" I begin, but she's already taken a few hesitant steps ahead. It's as if she too has seen the Black Rabbit and is following his path.

I pass by her quickly. *"Viola,"* I say again, and she flinches as if I just shook her awake. "You'll need to pick up the pace if we're going to catch him."

She nods and hurries alongside me.

The edges of the cemetery are lined with trees, their leafless limbs drooping low as if waiting to pluck the hat of a passerby. The Black Rabbit hurdles the fence and drops down onto the sidewalk. Hobbled but spry, he drags one foot as he rushes across the street.

We've gained ground, and I'm sure with a final burst I could clear the fence and tackle him before he reaches the other side of the road. But I halt abruptly and wrap my hands around two fence posts. Viola stops beside me.

There's something else out there.

The Black Rabbit darts behind a tall, spindly shadow in front of the row of glowing buildings. He peers back like a child taking shelter under the wing of a parent and flashes a sneer full of oversized human teeth.

I might have mistaken the shadow for one of the leafless saplings lining the quiet road, but it is wobbling, balancing on uneasy legs. The sleeves of a stretched wool sweater dangle almost all the way down to its laceless boots.

And on top of its head sits a jagged paper crown.

I narrow my eyes. "I know you," I whisper slowly. "But what *are* you?"

The shadow tilts his head on a boneless neck at the sound of my words, his cheek coming to rest on the folds of his crimson scarf. I see now that his face is ghastly white and entirely featureless, except for a garish red smile that appears to have been scrawled with a blunt crayon.

But his hollow black eye sockets extend a dark invitation.

Before I can accept, I'm interrupted by a bloodcurdling scream. I turn back to see the crowd of tourists at the other side of the cemetery. They gasp and point to the ground in alarm. Lizzy Prudence is gone.

The grave at her feet has opened up and swallowed her whole.

9

NIGHT TERRORS

Lizzy Prudence has broken character, uttering some colorful modern-day language as the paramedics cart her into a waiting ambulance. Her Victorian dress is hiked up past her knee, revealing an ankle swollen to twice its normal size. Aside from the bad foot and a few scrapes, she should be fine. The tourists mill around the double-decker bus, awaiting the arrival of a new guide. They'll have quite a story to tell their friends, but fortunately they've escaped the night unscathed too.

I step past the yellow police tape and stare down into the hole at my feet. It stinks of sour earth and ancient rot.

Lizzy didn't fall into an actual grave. The ground gave way and she found herself dangling inside one of the not-so-secret tunnels that crisscross under the North End of the city. These tunnels were all sealed up long before my time, and no one is completely sure of their original purpose. I've heard that a famous privateer used them to ferry illicit plunder from the harbor, but I wouldn't bet my wings on it.

I overhear the banter of a cemetery official and a policeman, who chat casually in front of the blinking blue-and-white lights of the officer's car. They seem content to chalk the sinkhole up to the unusually wet weather. I beg to differ.

Viola leans her head over the yellow tape without crossing it and whispers in my ear. "Did the Netherkin do that?"

I nod and Viola furrows her brow.

"But I don't think it was some sort of trap, if that's what you mean," I clarify. "It's just that these grounds have been disturbed by some serious comings and goings. More than just a little rain."

I look overhead. The night's otherworldly light show has come to an end, and the ungodly fist has disappeared like a passing cloud in a quick-moving storm. Big white crystals now fall from the sky. It's begun to flurry again.

More October snow.

I cast an eye over my shoulder at the row of buildings on the far side of the grounds. The Black Rabbit and his wobbly protector have disappeared, but a sinister static fills the air. The static exists on a frequency neither Viola nor the tourists can hear, but I pick it up the way a watchdog hears a whistle. It creeps along the cobblestones, lightly vibrating the trash cans set out on curbs like claws on a tabletop. The air is rich with a lingering sour stench, spoiling the smell of fresh bread from the bakery just down the street.

"I've found who I'm looking for," I grumble.

The stumbling specter I first mistook for a man in the Fens? The obscenely smiling scarecrow I just saw with the Black Rabbit outside the cemetery? They are indeed one and the same. Given his odd choice of headwear and limp-necked appearance, I can see why some dim-witted Netherkin might call him a Boneless King. But what exactly he *is* I can't put a finger on. He hums with the dark energy of the dead; I felt it much more strongly tonight than when I first met him. And yet there remains something organic—something *living*—pulsing inside him.

I'm tempted to rush into the row of buildings and flush him out from wherever he's now hiding, but I hesitate. If this Boneless King is the one calling these spirits, clearly he has some strong influence.

No, I'm *not* frightened—and I'm not sure why you keep thinking that. It's just that this might require a little more thought. Some careful planning. Besides, it wouldn't be fair to again leave Viola, who's looking paler than usual at the moment.

"Are you still feeling sick?" I ask her.

"I'll be all right."

"Come on," I say. "I'll walk you home."

"You don't need to do that."

I don't want to tell her that she shouldn't travel alone tonight. The static in the air—I haven't heard it this strongly in a very long time.

"It's okay," I reassure her. "I need to work up an appetite anyway." I glance around the burial ground and shake my head in disgust. "Netherkin," I growl. "This whole city has become a crawling buffet."

"Goyle, *no,*" she protests, more sharply. "I'd rather go on my own."

I'm taken aback. "Why?"

Viola adjusts her newsboy cap and pulls her coat tight around her. She pinches her lips together and seems to measure her words before speaking.

"Because I just met you. I don't want some monster, or *gargoyle,* or . . . whatever you are . . . following me to my house."

I'm blindsided. Her words sting, but I'm not about to show it. "Sorry" is all I mutter.

Viola tightens her grip on the violin case, takes three big strides away, then pauses.

"I'll come by to see you tomorrow," she adds quickly. "But please don't follow me. And remember, I can see you." She points her index and middle fingers to her own eyes and then directs them at me like a forked tongue. "I'll know if you do."

She hurries through the cemetery gates. Against my better judgment, I just watch her go.

I thrust my hands in my pockets and make the long walk back to my Domain. It's quiet enough to think. Unlike a certain overgrown city that shall remain nameless, this one has the decency to sleep. At this hour the streets are only populated by taxis and small packs of wandering practice-adults. One young couple has etched their initials and a heart in the dusting of snow on the sidewalk. With a sweep of my foot I send their valentine swirling into oblivion.

I'd say that my encounter with the Boneless King has left me feeling testy, but if I'm being honest, it's more than just that. Viola's words weigh heavily. The Twins and I often called one another names, but we never really *meant* them. Did I say something to offend her? It wasn't like I was pushy—*she's* the one who invited herself along. I was just trying to look out for her.

Maybe that's the problem. Not everyone wants to be looked after.

When I finally reach home I climb over the back wall of my Domain. From the courtyard, I see that the windows are brighter than usual. Except for the practice-adults, my Domain is not home to many night owls. I decide to check on my wards floor by floor.

There's a dim light under the crack of the Pandeys' apartment door, and behind it I can hear the normally happy couple arguing in hushed voices. In the stairwell on my way to the third floor I find a blond practice-adult weeping quietly. Her palms are pressed to mascara-smeared cheeks and a friend has an arm over her shoulder, trying to console her. They don't notice me as I slip past, of course. No loss. I'm of little use when it comes to tears anyway.

On the third floor I hear the old Korean lady snoring—she can sleep through a fire alarm without her hearing aid—but her cats are yowling and their anxious paws pad across linoleum as they bicker among themselves. From the end of the hallway I smell a hint of sage and venture down for a closer sniff. It's Miss Ada's apartment. I can tell she's burning a candle and sipping tea.

It seems that everyone is ill at ease tonight.

My next stop is the fourth floor.

The hallway is empty but something is amiss. Hetty's front door is cracked open, the bolt and chain loose. Sure, I keep a safe house, and in truth no unwanted prowler is going to intrude into my wards' apartments under my watch. But even so, nobody leaves their doors unlocked anymore. Hetty's mother probably had her hands full with Tomás and forgot to shut it. I hear him crying and I cringe. Not more tears. But this isn't the *Sob of the Soggy Diaper* or the *Bellow of the Empty Belly*. It's the inconsolable wail of a terror-stricken infant. I hear Mamita's urgent whispers of reassurance—the *March of the Desperate Mother*—as she roams from room to room, rocking him in her arms.

I inch toward the apartment but resist the urge to peek inside—child-rearing is none of my business. I'll just give the door a little nudge shut to spare her any undue worry come morning.

But before I can, a loud noise behind me makes my ears prickle.

There's a rumble of machinery in the bowels of the building, and the elevator shaft echoes with the clank and clatter of a rusting assembly line. Through the metal lattice, I see belts and conveyors moving.

I don't like this one bit. I didn't hear any of my wards come in. The grating of nails on a chalkboard fills my body.

The black mechanical beast comes to a stop. I ready myself. There's a pause, and the iron door slides open like the lid of a coffin. Inside, the elevator would appear empty to any of my wards.

But it's really not.

"You've *got* to be kidding me," I say.

Unlike the small Netherkin I found in the basement, this one consumes the entire elevator. It's as muscled and leathery as a rhino, but instead of four legs it crab-walks on hands and feet like a gymnast bent over backward. Its blocky head is mostly teeth, with a thick horn protruding between eyes that regard me with surprise from their upside-down perch. Two smaller arms and clawed hands protrude from the fiend's ribs, waggling toward the ceiling like antennas.

I clear my throat. "Do you know who I am, Netherkin?" I begin. "This is my Domain. I am the warden of—"

Oomph. It charges before I can finish, driving me into the wall.

"Spunky one, aren't—"

Oh! One of its smaller arms flails across my face, knocking me down. The formidable Netherkin snarls at me, then redirects its eyes toward Hetty's open door. It quickly lumbers for it.

"Not so fast," I command, and leap after it, grabbing its curly tail.

When the Netherkin turns to snap at me, I bring a fist down on its head, driving its face into the floor. It pinches its eyes tight in pain and I wrap my arms around it. Summoning my strength, I lift it off the ground and hurl it all the way down the hall. It crashes against the door of a corner apartment and lands upside down, its hands and feet wiggling like the legs of an overturned crab.

Oops, that move probably woke up the tenant. Do you ever hear strange thumps in the night? Well . . . never mind. Now's not the time.

The Netherkin scrambles to right itself. When it regains its feet, its broad body nearly fills the entire width of the hallway. It narrows its eyes and looks past me. Glancing over my shoulder, I see that Hetty's door is still open. I return my attention to the Netherkin and steady myself. There's no reasoning with this one. It looks like it's actually thinking about—

It charges again. This time I do the same and meet it head-on. The impact rocks us both, but I catch hold of its horn before I fall backward. I bellow a victory laugh and wrap my arms around its throat.

"Night-night, you—*ouch!*" I cry, and my hands fall away. I clutch my shoulder. The Netherkin has bitten right through my vest.

But once again, instead of continuing the fight, it pushes past me, making for Hetty's door.

Now all I see is red.

I tear after the Netherkin and throw myself at its legs like a cannonball. This time, before it hits the floor, I catch its body and sling its weight over my shoulder. With all my might, I haul it to the elevator and dump it inside, collapsing on top of it. The cage is thick with its stink, and we are a tangle of limbs, teeth, and claws.

But I'm unstoppable in close quarters. The Netherkin's size works against it as I bite away huge chunks of its leathery body. It thrashes and flails as I pummel, kick, and mash it against the elevator's walls, until eventually there's nothing left but a shapeless mass.

I step out of the elevator.

Yuck.

I'm covered in Netherkin. The elevator drips with what's left of it too.

The screeching chalkboard nails in my ears are gone, so I know that once again it's just me and my wards.

I turn toward the sound of Tomás's terrified sobs—still desperate and inconsolable. I'm sorry, little guy. I promise to be more careful from now on.

I make for the apartment door with every intention of easing it shut, but I stop in my tracks. A face appears around the frame.

Hetty stands in pajamas, the hem of her flannel bottoms falling short of her ankles. Her bare toes wiggle nervously on the hallway's cold floorboards. She blinks her wide eyes as she peers down the corridor. I try not to move. She seems to catch a glimpse of something and squints. I doubt she can see me, but even if she could, I can tell by her face it's not me she's looking for. After a moment, she steps back inside the apartment, pulling the door shut with a click.

I hear the bolt of the lock slide into place.

They're safe now, but don't try telling that to Tomás. His muffled cries echo down the hall, and I wonder what on earth is going on here.

I give the messy elevator one last look. I push a button and slide the door shut, sending it on its way.

I'm not about to clean *that* up—I'm the Night Warden, not the janitor.

10

ROUNDHEAD

It snowed all through the night. The stubborn storm of gentle flurries spread a white cloak over my wings and a cold carpet at my feet. A few more practice-adults eventually stumbled home and made their way to the roof, gleefully scraping together a pitiful snowman. He spent the early-morning hours slowly melting by my side.

Today, autumn has returned and the sad snowman has disappeared into nothingness. Only his wet stocking hat and a couple of bottle-cap eyes remain as evidence that he ever existed at all. I curse him. His soggy pretzel stick of a nose is sure to attract pigeons.

But the filthy birds are the least of my worries.

I peer down at the window of Hetty's apartment. I've been watching it all night and well into this late Sunday morning, but only now are Hetty and her family stirring. Tomás's restlessness has left them all tired and sluggish. If they only knew how much worse it could have been.

It's my fault, of course. I got sloppy. Let down my guard. Netherkin are like cockroaches. If you see one, it usually means more are out there, waiting to follow. I've squashed two this weekend already. I need to put an end to this now, before I have an infestation on my hands. My dance with the nasty brute in the elevator has left me hypersensitive. I'm feeling them all around me, lurking in every shadow. I imagine them scuttling in the alleyways even though I know they'd never venture out by day.

"Goyle?" a voice calls out. It's not coming from an alley or the street.

Viola is standing atop the roof on the building next to my Domain. She holds the handle of her violin case in both hands, her shoulders rounded. I'm relieved she made it home safely from Copp's Hill.

"Viola, what are you doing up there?"

"May I come over?" she asks hesitantly.

"Of course," I begin, but then realize I shouldn't sound so eager. After all, she wasn't very polite to me last night.

"I mean . . . if you *must*," I say more coolly.

The neighboring roof is several feet higher than my own, but the buildings on this block are pressed right up against each other, leaving very little gap between their walls. She plops down on her behind and swings her legs over the edge.

"Wait a minute," I say in alarm.

She scoots off, landing hard on the rooftop of my Domain.

I cringe. "Careful. You're not a Grotesque. Roof-hopping takes some getting used to."

Viola seems unfazed and walks over.

"Why can't you use the front door like everyone else?" I ask.

Viola shrugs, her eyes on the ground. "I wasn't sure you'd want to see me." When she looks up, her eyes blink hopefully under the brim of her wool cap.

I try to regain my stoic demeanor. I'm usually pretty good at it—I am made of stone, after all.

"Yes, well, I'm not so sure that I do," I huff.

Viola smiles. "I knew you'd forgive me."

Obviously not the look I was going for.

"I didn't say I *did*," I try.

Viola ignores my ill humor and sits down beside me. She sets the violin case next to her, dangles her boots over the edge, and smooths her leggings. I notice there are holes in each knee. It's not lost on me that she's been wearing the same tired-looking clothes for the past three days.

"Can you come out of there and sit with me?" she asks. "No offense, but I find it easier to talk with you when you don't look like some grim-faced monkey-dog-dragon monster."

"You know, I've always found the M-word offensive," I say. "Grotesques have feelings too."

She looks at me, confused.

"Monster," I clarify.

"I'm sorry, Goyle. I don't mean anything by it. And I apologize for saying it last night. I wasn't myself. The subway, the graveyard, the . . ." She pauses and shakes her head. "It was all more than I expected."

My feelings are still hurt, but I can understand how she might be overwhelmed. We Grotesques are a special breed. Fearlessness is in our nature.

"I'm *really* sorry," she says, and pats the rooftop next to her. "Will you please come out?"

"I don't know." I steal another glance at her violin case. Every time I see it, I want to peek inside. "Maybe you can play me a song," I say. "That would help me forgive you."

I'm surprised when Viola's hand darts to the case. "Oh, no," she objects. "I'm not good enough yet."

"I find that hard to believe," I say. "They don't admit just anyone to the Conservatory...."

She shakes her head. "No, no, no. Someday. But not today."

I frown. Viola raises an eyebrow. "Please sit with me?" she asks hopefully.

I sigh but accommodate her anyway. I guess I'm not the shrewdest negotiator.

Slipping free from my shell feels like wiggling out of scratchy, wet wool. If you don't do it right, it's as uncomfortable as getting the neck of a tight sweater stuck across your eyes. I sit next to her in my wisp form, dangling my own feet over the roof's edge and clasping my hands in my lap. We're quiet for a moment, and I catch Viola trying to peer under the shadows of my hood.

"That was quite a scene in the cemetery last night," she says.

I nod in agreement, tilting my head so that my hood shades my face.

"What do you suppose it was all about?" she asks.

I spent most of the night considering that very question. Memories are returning to me. The deafening static in the graveyard? The oppressive swirl of energy overhead? I *have* felt them before. A long time ago. They're part of a memory I spent years trying to bury. I did a good job of it, but now it's all swirling back.

"Hard to say for sure," I mutter. "Every now and then, things get shaken up. Have you ever heard of a hundred-year storm? One so strong you might experience it only once in a lifetime? It's like that. But when this kind of storm blows through, it can break down the walls between the living and the dead."

I glance up at an overcast sky that hasn't seen the sun in a week.

"That's what's happening now?" Viola asks.

"It certainly seems like it," I answer.

I don't mention that I've been through a storm like this once before. That was different. I wasn't alone. This time, I'm afraid there's not much I can do but hunker down and help my wards ride it out.

My eyes shift to Hetty's apartment. I spot her hanging something inside her window frame. It looks like a wind chime—delicate shards of jade and turquoise glass strung on fishing line.

Viola notices my gaze. "Who are they?" she asks.

"Her name is Hetty. She has a younger brother named

Tomás. He's the one you helped in the playground. They live with their mother."

Below us, Hetty balances atop a pink footstool as she positions the wind chime in her window. Her long wrists peek past her sleeves. She's still a child, but she's starting to outgrow everything around her. I hardly know Hetty, but I've seen enough to suspect that there's more to this young ward than meets the eye.

A bright flash of light surprises me. A sliver of aqua-colored glass has somehow caught a hint of light on this gloomy day and reflected it back in my face. I turn away, blinking.

"My wards had a bad night," I tell Viola, trying to clear my vision. "Hetty's family in particular."

Viola raises a quizzical eyebrow.

"Another Netherkin got into the building," I explain. "Made it all the way up to the fourth floor. It seemed pretty intent on getting into their apartment."

Viola's face tightens with concern.

"I know, I know," I say, trying to hide my embarrassment. "Look, they're crafty little pests. Sometimes one slips past even the best of us."

"Goyle, why would they be singling out that family?" she asks.

"I wouldn't say that they're actually singling them *out*—"

"How long have they lived here?" she interrupts.

"A couple of weeks, maybe. They just moved in."

"How many Netherkin have you discovered in your building since then?"

"Two."

Viola narrows her eyes. "And how many Netherkin do you normally get around here?"

"I don't know what you're implying, but I keep a clean Domain," I protest. No Netherkin has been foolish enough to trouble my wards in ten, fifteen years. Maybe longer.

"Sure, there was an imp that got stuck in a mailbox last winter," I confess. "But he was just hitching a ride in a Christmas package. He didn't seem any happier to be here than I was to find him. . . ."

I pause. Viola's stare is a chisel now. I guess I see her point.

"So maybe it's not just a coincidence," I concede. And, *yes,* I would have eventually drawn that conclusion on my own.

"What do you know about Hetty and her family?" Viola asks.

I rub my chin. "Well, Hetty's in fifth grade, I think.

Her mother's a nurse of some sort—sometimes she works long hours. Tomás is loud." I think harder. "They go through a lot of diapers. . . ."

Viola is waiting for more. I don't mention the unfortunate Ouija board incident, or Hetty's unusual interest in the comings and goings in the hallway the night before. It's suspicious behavior, but there's no need to give Viola the wrong impression until I make sense of it myself.

"I probably haven't gotten to know them as well as I should," I admit.

I look away and scowl at my neglect. I usually do a better job of getting acquainted with new wards. But truth be told, the Twins have dominated my thoughts and left me distracted from my duties.

"You need to get inside and find out what's going on in that apartment," Viola says.

"Maybe," I grumble. It's not a bad suggestion, but I'm not keen to admit it.

Viola is quiet. When I glance back over I find her watching me expectantly.

"So?" she says, after a moment.

"So what?"

"What are you waiting for?"

"You mean right now?"

"Do you have something else to do?"

She's more impatient than a leaky gable. Who's the Grotesque around here?

"Viola, just because you like to sit on rooftops doesn't mean you understand the complexity of my job," I remind her.

"What's so complex? You said yourself no one can see you. Pop on down there and snoop around."

I frown.

"Yes, well, here's the thing," I begin sheepishly. "I can't actually enter a ward's apartment unless I'm invited."

"What?" she says in surprise. "I thought this was your Domain?"

"It is. But that's sort of a rule."

"A rule? You have a rule book?"

"Call it an unwritten rule."

"I don't understand. You can't, like you're not supposed to, or you *can't*—like you're physically unable?"

"A bit of both."

Viola shakes her head. "I'm lost."

I sigh. "Have you ever stood on a high diving board and wanted to dive into a pool, but something comes over you and your feet won't budge?"

Viola glances at her boots swaying over the edge of the roof. "I'm not really afraid of heights."

I sigh again. "Yes, I get that. Me either. But you understand the idea, right?"

She just looks at me blankly. "You're afraid of Hetty's apartment?"

"*No*, I'm not *afraid*. I'm trying to describe the physical sensation. What about stage fright? You have to sing in front of an audience but you can't bring yourself to step through the curtain?"

She shrugs and pats the violin case. "Nope."

I slump my shoulders. Humans and their primitive minds.

"I don't like pie," she offers, scrunching her face. "Scary stuff."

I blink slowly in disbelief. "You're afraid of *pie*?"

"I burned my tongue on an apple pie when I was a little girl," she says, cringing at the memory. "Any kind of fruit-filled pastry terrifies me."

I can barely control my laughter.

"It's not funny, Goyle. My tongue was swollen up like a catcher's mitt. I had to drink my dinner through a straw for a whole week."

I choke back my amusement and compose myself.

"All right, I can work with that," I say. "Close your eyes."

"You're not going to tickle me, are you? I'm not crazy about that either."

"Just do it."

Viola pinches her eyes tight.

"Now, imagine that somebody has just put a piping-hot apple pie under your nose. It's fresh out of the oven."

Viola squirms.

"Smell the crust, the steaming filling. Here's a fork. Go on. Eat up. Take a big bite."

She squishes her face and shakes her head vigorously. I can see the discomfort in her puckered lips.

"*That's* what it would feel like if I tried to step into an apartment without being asked," I explain.

"Oh, that *is* awful." Viola reopens her eyes. "And if you're invited?"

I clap my hands together. "I'm in like a pig at a pie-eating contest."

Viola considers what I've told her.

"Well, it's simple enough, then," she declares after a moment. "We just need to get Hetty to invite you inside."

Viola and I stand in the middle of my rooftop. She looks me up and down in my wisp form. I try to stand up straight, smoothing my vest and straightening my hood self-consciously.

"We want Hetty to let you in, but she won't be able to see you, right?" she asks. "That could be a problem."

"I can make her, if I try really hard. Although I usually avoid that." I shift my feet under Viola's gaze. "Most people aren't all that eager to invite a creepy-looking wisp into their homes."

"Hmm, I see what you mean," she says, which makes me even less comfortable. She didn't have to agree so fast. "Maybe *I* could try instead?" she offers.

I put my hands on my hips. "Who's the Grotesque here? This is *my* Domain. You wouldn't possibly know what to look for once you were inside."

"Sorry," she says, backing down. "I was just trying to be helpful."

Viola circles around me, tapping a finger on her chin. I feel like a mannequin on display. She gestures in the air, outlining my human form.

"Is this all we have to work with, or can you change into something a little . . . cuter?" she asks.

"I'm not a magician, Viola," I say. "I can't just shapeshift willy-nilly. I can take the shape of a person, but otherwise I tend to be rather limited by my stone form."

"Another unwritten rule?" she asks, disappointed.

I glower and nod.

She glances over at my stone shell. I think my regal

wings, strong haunches, and watchful eyes are all rather charming, but the look on Viola's face tells me otherwise. "So what else you got?" she asks skeptically.

"Bat?"

"No," she says flatly.

"Monkey?"

"As much as I'd love to see you peel a banana with your feet, that might look a bit out of place in the city."

I think about it a bit more, then snap my fingers. "How about this?"

I contort my face, and my neck begins to stretch. My arms morph into two great capes of feathers and my nose stretches into a long beak. My feet lengthen into sharp talons.

Viola takes a step away in disgust as I stretch my enormous black wings with pride. Not bad for my first attempt at a vulture.

"That's horrible!" she gasps. "Stop it. Change back."

I strut around, bobbing my bald pink head. "If you knew how much I detest feathered creatures, you'd appreciate the effort," I say.

"Seriously, Goyle, you're hopeless. Can't you come up with anything warm and fuzzy?"

I cluck my black bird tongue and think some more. I wrack my memory for something I can pull off in somewhat-convincing fashion. Then it hits me. I recall a pet that was quite fashionable during the time of my Maker. It should do the trick.

The vulture begins to shrink. I replace its wings and talons with four short legs. The long beak retracts until it becomes a stubby, wet nose. My feathers are now a coat of trim black fur, highlighted by a nice patch of white around my muzzle and on my round, pettable tummy. My body has the dimensions of a stocky little barrel.

I blink my huge brown eyes at Viola.

"Roundhead," I say, with a smile that reveals a chipped canine. "These days, you'd call me a Boston terrier."

Viola pauses and looks me over. She doesn't jump with enthusiasm, but at least she's not disgusted.

"So what do you think?" I ask. I turn around, flash my rump, and wag my curly little tail.

She sighs and offers a reluctant nod. "Well, have you ever heard the expression *so ugly it's cute*? I'd say you nailed it."

11

WHITE LIES

"Pastrophobia," I say as I trot around the roof, trying to get comfortable with my four new legs.

"What?" Viola asks. She's sitting cross-legged, her violin case in her lap.

"Pastrophobia," I repeat, impressed with myself for having remembered the term. "That's what you have."

"What on earth are you talking about?" she asks. There's an impatience in her voice as she watches me circle her.

"Pastrophobia is the fear of pies and baked goods," I say.

"You're making that word up."

I shake my head, my terrier jowls jiggling. "Nope."

"Where did you learn that?"

"The library. It's been around as long as I have."

"You do a lot of reading?" she asks, surprised.

"I prefer comics. But '92 was a particularly quiet year. I started memorizing the dictionary to pass the time. Made it through the *E*s, *G*s, *I*s, and *P*s."

"You didn't start in alphabetical order?"

"Where's the fun in that?" I ask.

She just shakes her head.

"The library's a great place," I add. "There used to be some imps in the cooking section."

I still remember their strange honey-and-sugar taste to this day. The Twins insisted they were fairies. Or guardian angels, not that I believe in such things. I smack my lips at the memory.

"*Used* to be," I emphasize.

"Goyle, you've been at this for an hour. Don't you think it's about time you find your way down to Hetty's apartment?"

"This form takes some getting used to," I say. "I'm not going to make a very convincing dog if I accidentally start walking on two legs. Besides, I can't very well go gallivanting around the halls like some lost puppy."

I cock my head and give her a wink of my round eye.

"*Gallivant.* Do you like that one? It means to travel or roam about for fun."

"Fascinating," Viola says without enthusiasm.

"I need to try tomorrow when I can find Hetty by herself," I explain. "Her mother will just complicate things. Hetty sits in the courtyard every day after school. She doesn't do much. Just sketches in a notebook or stares at the walls for hours until her mother gets home." I pause. "It's almost like she doesn't want to be in the apartment alone."

"Tomorrow?" Viola asks, unfolding her legs. "What if the Netherkin come tonight?"

I stop, stand upright on my hind legs, and cross my forepaws. "What are you saying? That I'm stalling?"

"No, of course not," she says, and looks away. I see her fidget with the clasps of the violin case. "I'm sure you know what you're doing. I was just trying to be helpful. . . ."

Viola offers a small smile. I return a sarcastic but not unkind grin that reveals a hint of teeth.

"Goyle," Viola says, "even as a dog I can see the little scar over your eye. And your tooth is still chipped." She glances back at my shell, which mirrors the old injuries. "How did it happen?"

I close my mouth and drop back down onto all fours.

"Just a little tumble—a long time ago," I say, tight-lipped. I run my tongue along the broken canine.

That memory I've struggled so long to forget has come crashing back again. I notice that my short tail has involuntarily slumped between my legs. I quickly shake the pesky thing to life.

"Nothing serious," I fib.

Viola studies my stubby face, as if deciding whether or not to believe me. I don't think she does.

"Well, I guess I should get going," she says, slowly pushing herself to her feet. Maybe she's noticed my sudden change in mood.

"That's probably a good idea," I agree—probably too quickly. I wonder if I was supposed to stop her. "I mean, you never know when someone might wander up and wonder what you're doing here. Where are you off to?"

She adjusts her wool cap and picks up the violin case.

"I've got a rehearsal. Nearly forgot all about it."

"On a Sunday?"

"We've got a fall concert coming up." There's another adjustment of her cap.

"Oh," I say. "Maybe I could come listen?"

"Yeah, maybe," she says, peering out over the rooftops. "I'll let you know." She moves to leave, then hesitates.

"I'll stop by tomorrow, Goyle. Don't put off checking the apartment for too long. It could be really important."

Before I can get testy again, or explain that I know a thing or two about minding my wards, she hurries off, exiting by the neighboring roof.

I sigh and sit on my haunches, scratching an itch behind my ear with one of my hind legs. Viola's questions may have soured my mood, but now that she's gone, I'm not relieved by the solitude. I run my long pink tongue over my chipped tooth again. It's not that I'm *vain*—just a little sensitive about it. Viola couldn't possibly have known why.

And I suppose I didn't have to lie.

The Twins and I never lied to one another. Even if we wanted to, it's tough to keep secrets when you've been sitting around the same building for a hundred years— everyone always knows what you're doing and where to find you.

I pad to the edge of my roof and drop down beside my stone shell. I stare out at the skyline. A black-hooded predator is perched atop the glass tower on Boylston Street. Below it, a fat gray pigeon flutters leisurely through the air. In the blink of an eye, the predator dives straight down, wings pinned at its sides. The pigeon explodes in midair, feathers fluttering like snowfall as the peregrine falcon returns to its perch high above.

As you know, I'm no fan of feathered creatures. But maybe these falcons weren't the worst addition to our rooftops.

I cast my eyes toward a different row of buildings in the shadow of the tower. Shorter and older, they predate the metal mountains that have grown up around them.

Those buildings are part of another memory. The one I've tried so hard to forget.

The recollection remains distant, but now that it's back, it gnaws and haunts me worse than the bite of any Netherkin.

12

THE GREAT WAR

The old memory tumbles into focus. The world is at war. And so are we. Men are being shipped by boat to fight overseas, but for us the battle is here on our streets and rooftops.

An unexpected October snowstorm has paralyzed the city. Fortunately, it came by night, and most residents remain huddled in their buildings. The streets are deserted—empty of the horses and buggies that still share the road with primitive automobiles.

I'm perched on a rooftop that's not my own. The brownstone is one of many along a street of ornate buildings modeled after a famous boulevard in France. Wallace and Winnie are at my side. Across the wide roadway, I see our other friends at their posts among the gables, snow collecting on mighty stone shoulders.

We're not wisps, but hardened granite warriors. Those of us with wings have taken flight and assumed new posts. Those without, fortify the streets and subway tunnels. And now we wait.

Our enemies are coming. We can feel them.

I look overhead, where thick clouds swirl black and blue, squatting over the city like a smothering blanket. There are no glass-and-steel towers. The buildings are pillars of brick and mortar that look like failing tent poles trying to prop up the canopy of gloom.

We hear the calls and cries of our comrades up ahead on the front lines, their voices nearly drowned by the deafening static that fills the air. Today's battle hasn't gone as well as expected. Our enemies will be here soon.

None of us knows exactly who started this war. Or why. There have been whispers and gossip, of course—of a mysterious and powerful warlord who's risen from the earth and summoned an army of undead soldiers to do his bidding. While there are always a few Netherkin lurking outside our Domains or hounding our wards, this is entirely different. Seldom do they unite in such force. All we really know for sure is that battles such as this have been waged on and off throughout the centuries. Nobody is here to lead us or explain the stakes, but we understand that the consequences of failure will be grave ... and will upend our wards' world. Our elders throughout Europe have defended many onslaughts. For us here, the *terrible children*, this one's our first. I'm glad I don't have to fight it alone.

"How are you feeling, Penhallow?" Winnie asks, turning her head. Wallace's eyes remain fixed on the road.

I think before answering. I'm alert but exhausted. Like I haven't slept in days. I know the fatigue will be crushing when this is all over, but the excitement makes my tail twitchy.

"Alive," I say.

Winnie gives me a tight smile and flexes a claw. "Me too."

It's then that the first swarm of the Netherkin appears at the far end of the avenue. So many gather that they are soon crawling over each other like a giant colony of black ants. The collective mass of their bodies begins to rise up like a wave, before cresting and spilling toward us.

The air goes sour with their stench.

We're outnumbered a hundred to one, but that won't deter us. We may not know who started this war, but we have no choice but to win it.

I hear the flap of heavy wings as gray forms take flight. I beat my own wings, feel them catch the breeze, and push my claws off the edge. Our small squadron of Grotesques hovers together in formation for a moment, before we dive down and throw ourselves into the sea of Netherkin.

The sky disappears as I'm surrounded by their creeping swarm. Best-laid plans and tactics are abandoned in the chaos. The melee itself is all a fleeting blur now, but when the conflict's over, we've done our job.

It's not without cost.

The battle leaves a wasteland of fallen and battered friends. Some who survive are too weak to return to their Domains and can only collapse on the streets, finding themselves buried in snowdrifts so deep they won't be uncovered until spring. Helpless and hibernating, they'll be smashed into movable pieces, then shoveled up and collected in trucks and wheelbarrows, dumped into quarries or ground into asphalt. It's an inglorious ending for heroes who fought so bravely.

I'm one of the lucky ones. I'm able to stagger back to my Domain before exhaustion overtakes me. I just want to drag myself to my roof and sleep, but in my absence, something has gone terribly wrong.

There are Netherkin here.

We may have thwarted their army, but a few stragglers

remain fragmented across the city, looting and pillaging before retreating into the depths from which they came.

I've no time or energy for stealth. I crash through the window of the apartment where I sense them. My stone form does real damage to the glass-and-wood frame, but my wards will just assume it was the windstorm. The two shapes I find inside the small room are familiar. It's been a while since I've last seen them, but not long enough.

The *One with the Horns.*

The *One in the Hat.*

Their shadow bodies huddle over a crib. It's not the same crib or baby as the first time I encountered them; that one is long since grown and moved away. But for undead fiends like the One with the Horns and the One in the Hat, any infant will do. Shapeshifters, they're masters of guile and stealth, and their prizes are priceless and irreplaceable. When the Shadow Men look up, the One in the Hat is clutching a tiny blue bundle greedily in his arms. The shimmery sphere pulses meekly in his tight grip, its softly glowing edges as delicate as a dandelion's fluff.

I lunge at them, but it feels like I'm carrying the weight of an entire building on my shoulders. They easily outpace me, and I'm still far behind them as they flee from the apartment and down the hallway. They leap into the elevator shaft, the stolen bundle tucked under the shadowy arm of the One in the Hat. I dive in after them. I can no longer lift my wings to fly, so I climb desperately, my claws tearing cables and gears.

I follow the Shadow Men all the way to the roof. It's my last hope to stop them. But they've reached the parapet by the time I burst through the ceiling in a cloud of dust and broken bricks. With my last gasp, I hurl myself at them to snare their legs.

But I fall short. And hard. So hard I break my tooth and smash my brow.

The One in the Hat realizes they've got me beat. I hear him snicker as he glances back over his shoulder with a narrow slit of an eye. Then they both disappear off the edge of the roof with the little blue sphere.

They leave me as crushed as the Grotesques left behind on the streets.

I'm helpless and can no longer move. Soon my fatigue will overtake me and I'll have no choice but to sleep for a very long time. I can't make it inside the apartment for one last look in the crib. I know the baby still lies there, wiggling fitfully in his sleep. They didn't take his body, but they've made off with a piece of him that's far more precious. His life will be one of sickness and sadness, of fear and depression. Neither his parents nor his doctors will ever know why.

Unfortunately, I will. And I've never forgotten. I wasn't there when my ward needed me most.

That's the story I couldn't share with Viola.

The story of how I got my scars.

And my memory of the last time the city swirled in darkness and hummed with the threat of permanent night.

13

Clover

I've adopted my new canine form again. Wads of old gum hover precariously above me. White, gray, orange, brown. What flavor is *brown*? I shake my head in disappointment. My wards can be a disgusting bunch. I lie flat on my belly, furry chin resting on my front paws.

I hide under the bench in the courtyard of my Domain. It's mid-afternoon on Monday and our sad little oasis is deserted, which is typical for this time of day. But Hetty should be home from school any minute. After she arrives, she'll wander out here and sit on this bench. She won't do anything except stare at the gray clouds, watch, and wait. I'm not sure why, but she's done it every day since she moved in.

I expect this will be my best chance to catch Hetty alone. I hope I'm right. Adults complicate things ... and tend to frown upon taking in strange creatures off the street.

From inside, I hear the jingle of keys and the heavy front door of my Domain. Footsteps approach the back exit of the building.

I ready myself—it's time for my big reveal. This part is tricky. I puff out my jowls and belly. I push my insides against the contours of my wisp form. Imagine pinching your nose just in time to trap an enormous sneeze. It's about as comfortable as that.

I hear a girl's voice and the rear door of my Domain squeaks open.

I push harder, until it feels like my ears might burst. My whiskers twitch and my round eyes bulge even wider than they already look. I only stop when my ears are ringing so loudly that I can't possibly take any more. Finally, I gasp in relief. That should do it.

I glance down, where the contours of my wisp body have become flushed with color and life. All right, so maybe they're mostly just black and white, but it's not like I'm masquerading as a peacock. I've done a fine job, if you ask me, and the real point is that I should now be visible to anyone who looks my way.

Sneakers walk into the courtyard and step into view. Now's my chance.

I creep out from my hiding place, plastering on the meekest, most harmless expression I can muster.

Uh-oh.

The girl standing in front of me isn't Hetty. She's tall and thin, with a backpack slung over her shoulder, but she's blond—and much older. She's gabbing into a little white headset that dangles from her ear while quickly plucking the buttons of an impossibly thin telephone in her hands. I recognize her as the weepy practice-adult from the stairwell this past weekend.

"He still hasn't apologized yet," she laments to the friend in her ear. "I mean, who does that? It's not like we—" Her voice stops as she glances up and catches sight of me.

"Ohhhhh," she drawls, in the tone of someone who has just laid eyes on a sleeping baby or playful kitten.

Oh, I grunt to myself, in the tone of someone who has just discovered a Netherkin hair in his soup.

"Sarah, there's the cutest little dog in our courtyard," she says with a smile. "I don't know, some sort of bulldog, maybe. Hi, boy," she coos, in a high falsetto voice.

She crouches and steps closer. I backpedal on my paws.

"He doesn't have a collar. Maybe he's a stray. Are you a stray, little guy?"

I glance under the bench. Maybe if I hide there again she'll go away.

"I can't just leave him here. What time are you coming home?" she's saying. It's getting hard to tell who she is talking to. "Would you like to come home with me?" she asks, looking my way.

Nope, that won't be necessary.

The practice-adult reaches as if she might pick me up.

I summon my ferocious animal voice and bellow an intimidating, wolflike bark to keep her at bay.

It comes out as an excitable yip.

"He wants to play!" she gushes into her phone.

Oh, bricks.

I turn tail and run. I scamper across the courtyard but she follows, babbling to both me and the invisible friend chattering in her ear. Fortunately, my short legs are quick. When she goes left, I go right. When she follows right, I pivot left. But the practice-adult is relentless. After several minutes of this nonsense, I realize I have no other option. I have to get rid of her before Hetty arrives.

I stop and let her get close. Then, when she's in arm's

reach, I squat. And deposit a little present for her right on the concrete. It smells like Netherkin.

The practice-adult halts abruptly and her face contorts in a look of horror. I'm not proud of any of this, but sometimes we do what we must.

"*Gross!*" she squeals. "Gross, gross, gross," she repeats, hurrying away as if my gift might grow legs and chase her.

I scamper behind a planter and watch her go.

"Oh my god, Sarah," I hear her muttering as she flees. "He just took a big—"

The door clicks shut behind her.

I carefully peek out from between the leaves of a potted fern. I'm alone, but this isn't going as well as I'd hoped. Maybe I need to come up with a better plan.

Unexpectedly, the door opens again, and I quickly duck back behind the planter, afraid she's changed her mind.

But the girl who appears this time isn't chattering to any invisible friends. Her hair bounces in loose ringlets that match her dark eyes. She wears a green raincoat and rubber boots that she taps nervously as she takes a seat on the bench.

What a relief. It's Hetty. She pulls her backpack off her shoulder and holds it in her lap, her fingers drumming the buckle and strap as her eyes dart around, studying the walls and windows above her.

Well, it's now or never. No sense waiting for another practice-adult to make an unwelcome appearance.

I venture from my hiding place once again, offering the same meek face that was so effective before. I creep close before Hetty finally looks down and sees me, and when she does she looks surprised but not startled. She doesn't squeak or squeal, but her face brightens. She gently extends a palm.

I guess I'm supposed to sniff it.

I lean in and twitch my nose. Yuck. Peanut butter and fifth-grade germs. I do my best not to appear disgusted.

Satisfied that I won't bite, she reaches out to scratch my head. I quickly lurch away so I don't blow my cover. Hetty may be able to see me now, but remember, I still can't touch or be touched by the living.

"I'm sorry, you must be frightened," she says. Her voice is soft and soothing. "What's your name, little guy?"

Penhallow, I'd like to reply. But Hetty's not some preschooler who believes in fairy tales. I'm pretty sure a talking terrier would earn a call to the dogcatcher.

"I know, it's not like you can tell me," she says with an understanding smile. "So for now, maybe I'll call you ..." She pauses to think. "Clover."

Oh, that's *awful.* I think I'd even prefer Goyle to that. I squish my face into what I hope is a mopey look of disapproval.

"You look hungry, Clover."

Not exactly the expression I was going for. This is going to take some practice.

Hetty checks over her shoulder to confirm we're alone. "I don't know where you came from," she says. "They don't allow dogs in the building."

Her tone tells me it's not a rule she approves of.

"I've never seen you before, and I sit here almost every day."

I cock my head. Yes, I've been wondering about that. Among other things.

"We had a little garden at my old apartment," Hetty says. "My dad always used to wait for me there when I came home from school. It didn't matter if it was raining or snowing, I knew he'd always be in that garden . . . waiting." She glances around the courtyard with a shrug. "It's not the same, but sometimes I like to sit here, and just . . . remember."

Hetty shivers and pulls the collar of her raincoat tighter around her neck. "It's getting colder every day, though," she says, and casts an eye my way. "You must be cold too."

I muster a sad little whimper, then plop down on my

side. I roll over so she can see my adorable belly in need of love and scratching. I see her face melt, and a look of quiet rebellion flashes in her eyes.

"Do you want to come inside?" she whispers. "Just for a minute. I can get you something to eat."

Now this is more like it. I told Viola I'd be irresistible. *So ugly it's cute,* my tail. I wag it affirmatively.

Hetty pats her thigh and gestures for me to follow her to the door. "Come on," she coaxes. I hesitate so that I don't seem too eager, then follow her inside.

I've never seen my Domain from this perspective before. As my claws click across the tiles, I notice that the grout could use a good scrubbing. And my wards should really learn to use the doormat to wipe their feet.

Hetty checks the entryway to be sure we're alone, then hurries for the elevator and presses the button. Somewhere above us the black beast rumbles to life.

No way. Not under the best of circumstances. And definitely not after what I left in there the other night.

I scurry toward the door to the stairwell instead.

"You don't have to be afraid. It's just an elevator," she says.

But I'm adamant, and eventually she shrugs her backpack over her shoulder. We head up the three flights of stairs.

A quick check of the hallway, and Hetty ushers me toward her apartment. She removes her keys and unlocks it.

"Come on," she whispers, with another pat on her thigh. She doesn't need to ask me twice.

I sit on the linoleum while Hetty rummages through the cupboards in search of something a stray dog might like to eat. The apartment is what I expected. It's simply furnished; a well-worn sofa is joined by a small bouncing chair and a netted playpen designed to corral a wandering one-year-old. A calendar and pencil sketches decorate the refrigerator and a few dishes from this morning's breakfast line the sink. Cardboard boxes that still await unpacking have been pushed into corners. Overall, it's a friendly sort of clutter.

But there's a foul odor in the air that I didn't expect. And I don't mean Captain Poopy-Pants's diaper pail. My sense of smell is even keener than a real dog's, and the unpleasant scent cuts through the aroma of baby powder and a bouquet of fading lilies.

Hetty places a cup of water and a cereal bowl full of stinky brown mush on the floor in front of me. I lean over and put my nose in it. It smells like the fishermen's push-carts at Haymarket on a hot Saturday afternoon, but the bowl's not the source of the troubling odor either.

"Cod, pork liver, brewer's yeast, carrageenan . . ." Hetty is squinting and reading the label of the emptied tin can between her fingers. "Calcium pan-toe-thee-nate," she sounds out, and frowns. "Sorry, we don't have any dog food. This was for our cat. It died."

With a diet like that, I can see why.

Hetty looks at me expectantly. I want to investigate that other smell—the one coming from down the hall—but she's insistent that I eat something first. This is a problem. I'm not built to digest stuff like this. Netherkin, imps, the occasional poltergeist, for sure. But if I eat that bowl of slop, I'm going to pay for it tomorrow, and probably the next day too.

"Go on, just try it, Clover," she urges gently. "It's better than being hungry."

It seems there's no way around this. If I'm going to earn her trust, I need to accept her offering. The things I do for my wards.

I steady myself and try to imagine that the fishy muck is a bowl of those honey imps from the library. If the Twins could see this, they'd never let me hear the end of it. I close my eyes.

Imps, imps, imps. Here goes.

I plunge my stubby snout into the cat food and gulp it up in huge mouthfuls, swallowing it down before it can linger on my tongue. I tear into it ferociously, and thanks to my vivid imagination, the bowl is cleaned in just seconds. I look up in shock, blinking my bulgy eyes in surprise.

Cat food . . . is . . . *delicious*!

Hetty looks just as stunned as me. Maybe I was a bit *too* convincing.

I see her check the clock on the wall. She takes her backpack from the kitchen chair and slings it over her shoulder. I don't think the backpack needed mending, but it's covered with sewn-on patches—logos of her school's sports teams, bands I've never heard of, and a black four-leaf clover that might explain her poor choice of dog's names.

"See, don't you feel better?" she says. "Come on, I'll show you my room."

Hetty starts down the hall and I don't hesitate to take her cue. I jog in front of her, wary now. As we near the door to her room my ears perk up. The smell is growing stronger. Strong enough to identify.

It's the acrid stench of danger.

And it's coming from Hetty's bedroom.

She reaches for the doorknob and I position myself at

her feet, creating a fearsome barrier between Hetty and whatever's lurking on the other side.

"You're an eager one, Clover," she says with a smile. "Look at that tail go."

I try to still my wagging nub of a tail without much success. I bare my teeth, ready to pounce.

As soon as she cracks the door, I hurl myself at a gangly, freakish brute before he knows what hit him.

14

Indigo Child

A stuffed orange orangutan with a dangling tongue tastes my wrath. He's lounging on a plush yellow chair sized for a young child.

"Don't eat Mr. Jum-Jums!" Hetty calls in alarm.

My paws sink into his soft belly as I land on him. He offers the high-pitched yelp of a squeak toy but puts up no defense.

Hmm. Mr. Jum-Jums doesn't seem to be the culprit.

I dismount the stuffed animal and bury my nose in the floor, navigating quickly through a maze of unpacked boxes. I check under the bed, then dart out the other side.

I jump onto the mattress, investigating under the pillows and through the folds of Hetty's floral-print comforter.

Hetty giggles. "Go on, you can explore."

Strange. I can feel a darkness here, but I can't quite put my nose on it. I narrow my eyes at her brightly painted desk. It's cluttered with loose papers and pencils. A fat black moor goldfish swims in endless circles around a small bowl. I hop on the chair so I can take a closer look. The goldfish's telescoping eyes pause and stare, unblinking, at my own. The scent of danger grows stronger.

"Do you like Fin?" Hetty asks, coming over to me.

Not particularly. Although he smells vaguely like the delicious cat feast I just devoured, he's not what I'm looking for either. But I'm getting closer.

"The building doesn't allow dogs," she reminds me with a wink. "So he was my housewarming pet."

Hetty tries to squeeze onto the chair next to me and I'm forced to retreat again, fearful of blowing my disguise. She's disappointed, but understanding. I take a few steps away and drop myself down with Mr. Jum-Jums.

"I've had this desk since I was a little girl," Hetty explains. She rubs her palm over its surface. "It used to be plain brown but my dad helped me repaint it."

Hetty blinks in silence for a moment, then reaches into

a pocket of her backpack and removes a tiny, fragile key. I notice now that the middle drawer houses a small keyhole. She moves to unlock it but stops at a distant sound.

I hear it too. Down the hall, the locks on the apartment door rattle open. There's a jangle of keys landing on the counter, the tap of heels, and the gurgles and squawks of an impatient baby brother.

"My mother's home early," Hetty whispers, and stuffs the key into a pocket of her jeans.

She quickly rises to her feet and turns to me in earnest. "Clover, you have to be quiet." She places her finger to her lips. "If my mother finds out you're in here, you'll have to go."

"Hetty, are you home?" her mother's voice calls from the kitchen.

Hetty takes a careful step toward the door. "Coming, Mamita," she calls back, and turns to me once more. "Quiet, okay? You have to make yourself invisible."

Little does Hetty know that *invisible* is my specialty.

The hours pass as Hetty's family tackles their evening tasks. My keen ears gather that Mamita has come home early to spend some extra time with Hetty. Unfortunately, she's picked a day when Hetty has other things on her mind. Hetty checks on me several times, and I get the sense that she is being extra-cooperative for her mother. There's a shower for her and a bath for Tomás. Dinner and cleanup. Then Hetty struggles through her homework. Her mother tries to help, but she's torn between Hetty's long division and her brother's fussing. From what I overhear, it seems Hetty is having some trouble in school. She hasn't been sleeping and it's hard for her to concentrate.

All these chores take time, but it gives me a chance to explore every nook and cranny of Hetty's room. My canine form proves useful, as it's much easier to get into the closet and hamper, sniff under the radiator, and squeeze behind her bureau. I can't reach the wind chime hung in front of her window, but I'm close enough now to get a much better look. Delicate shards of sea glass are strung on clear fishing line, their frosted shades of aqua, green, and seafoam brightening the shadows cast by the grime-caked fire escape just outside.

But despite my careful investigation, I don't find the source of the dangerous energy that haunts this room. I've checked everywhere except for one stubborn place.

I can't get inside that locked drawer.

Eventually it's bedtime, and I lie completely silent under the bed while Mamita walks Hetty through their nighttime ritual. I wonder if, somewhere else, Viola is going through a similar process at this very moment. The room is dark except for the glow of the little lamp on Hetty's desk. There's a collection of creams and essential oils on her nightstand. Mamita rubs them gently into Hetty's skin as she tucks her in, telling her they should help with her insomnia. Mamita pushes a button on a small machine on the floor and it hums to life, broadcasting a steady tone of soft white noise to drown out the street traffic.

"Let's have a good night, okay?" Mamita whispers as she gently lays the comforter over Hetty's shoulders.

"Okay," Hetty whispers back.

"No wandering the hall. If you wake up, just stay in your bed and try to think happy, relaxing thoughts."

"I'll try," Hetty assures her.

Mamita pauses. It seems that she wants to linger, to stay and lie with Hetty until she drifts off to sleep. But Tomás is stirring in the other bedroom. His muffled calls are sure to turn into bellowing cries if he's ignored for too long.

I hear the creak of the bed as Mamita gets up, and together she and Hetty recite a little poem.

Trust in the Fairies
Who watch through the night.
Trust in their magic,
The moon and its light.
Just close your eyes
And wish on a star,
The Fairies will guard you
Wherever you are.

Fairies. They always get all the credit. No one ever writes poems about Grotesques.

From my hiding spot, I can now see Mamita's back as she approaches the desk.

"Please leave the light on," Hetty says, and her mother stops. Mamita's shoulders slump ever so slightly, as if she was expecting but is still disappointed by the request.

"Of course, darling," she says.

Mamita moves toward the door, where I catch a glimpse of her face. Her features are dark and pretty like Hetty's, but there are tired circles under her eyes and a hint of sadness on her lips.

Tomás's cries are growing louder.

"I love you, Hetty," Mamita says.

"Love you too."

Mamita pulls the door halfway shut as she goes, leaving it ajar.

"Mamita," Hetty calls, and her mother pauses and pokes her head back inside.

"You can close the door."

Mamita seems surprised but not displeased. She offers a tired smile.

"Good night, my Indigo Child," she says.

"Good night," Hetty replies, and the door closes with a gentle click.

Hetty lies completely still. Her mother is lingering just outside—I can see the shadows of her slippers under the crack of the door. My guess is that she's listening, waiting for a final request. But after an extended silence, her footsteps pad away, the hallway goes dark, and I hear her own bedroom door click shut as she takes up her vigil with Tomás.

The bed creaks as Hetty springs up. Her eager face appears on the floor just inches from my own, peering under the bed on her hands and knees.

"Okay, Clover, you can come out."

I carefully creep forward on my belly, stretching and shaking the dust from my short coat of fur.

Hetty retrieves some old newspapers she's stashed in a

corner. She lays them carefully in front of me on the floor. I blink slowly. Does she expect me to read them?

"I'm sorry," she whispers. "I can't take you outside for a walk, and I know you must be ready to burst. Try to use those, okay?"

So undignified. Fortunately, they won't be necessary. *Yes*, I know there's the matter of the deposit I left in the courtyard. But those were desperate circumstances. Let's not bring it up again.

Hetty hesitates, pressing her ear to the closed door. Satisfied that her mother has gone to bed, she carefully retrieves something from the pocket of the folded jeans laid over the back of her chair. It's the tiny key. She heads for the desk.

This is it! I prepare myself without seeming too eager. Whatever's in there, I'll be ready for it.

Hetty unlocks the drawer with the tiniest of clicks. The wooden drawer scrapes open, rough and coarse. Before I can stop her, she reaches inside.

Out comes a bulging, musty, purple-scaled . . . *journal*?

Hetty brings it to her bed and sits cross-legged, holding it in her lap. She loosens the elastic band around the journal and opens its thick reptilian cover. I join her on the bed and study it suspiciously.

"Oh, you can read, can you?" she says, amused.

Actually, *I can.* The library, remember? I'm quite *erudite*—look that one up.

"I'm sorry, I'm sure you're a very smart boy," Hetty says with a smile. "This is my journal. I've kept it for a while now, ever since my, ever since . . ." Her voice trails off. She sighs. "The school counselor said I should write down my feelings. He said it might help me . . . *process* my emotions."

Interesting. Feelings have always struck me as something to be avoided. Or ignored. I've found that they can be distracting. And inconvenient.

"Not that I put a lot of stock in what the counselor says, if that's what you're thinking," Hetty continues. "He's much older than me and both of his parents are *still* alive. But my father used to keep a journal. Lots of them, actually. He never let me read them, but sometimes he'd read a passage or two out loud at bedtime. Usually something nice he'd written about me, or Tomás, or Mamita. So I figured it couldn't hurt."

I look at the pages as Hetty flips through them. She prints in all capital letters. A lot of them are backward. There are little things taped here and there: a dried flower; a newspaper clipping; a black business card frayed around the edges. But mostly what I see are pencil sketches. Her gray and white scratchings form vague images.

She turns back to the first sheet of paper, which serves as a cover page. Written in large static letters are the words *Confessions of an Indigo Child*.

"My father used to call me his Indigo Child," she says, placing a finger on the words. "So I thought that would make a good title."

Hetty's words are warm and gentle. Touching, even. So why does this child's tome remind me of a purple-scaled crocodile lying in wait, its pages stinking of danger?

"I never got to say goodbye to him," she says. "But the past few nights ... someone has been whispering to me in the dark. I'd say it's in my dreams, but I know I'm not really asleep."

My ears twitch. I don't like the sound of that one bit. But Hetty's voice brightens with optimism when she confides, "I think it might be him."

She's quiet, blinking slowly.

"Don't be scared, Clover," she says after a moment, and closes the journal. "He means us no harm. I think he just wants to tell me something. Come on, let's close our eyes and try to sleep. Maybe you can meet him yourself."

I find it strange how Hetty almost seems to know what I'm thinking. She can't possibly hear me, of course. But even if she *could*, she definitely doesn't understand me.

It's not *me* I'm frightened for.

15

STATIC

I'm curled up at the foot of Hetty's bed. I can tell by the gentle rise and fall of her comforter that she's finally drifted off, her breathing quiet and steady. Traffic has died down outside and the noise machine churns along, doing an admirable job of filtering exterior distractions. I've been on high alert for hours, and yet nothing unusual has disturbed us. As ominous as the purple journal smelled, I'm fairly certain it's not about to grow fangs and chew its way out of the desk drawer.

Hetty's peaceful slumber is contagious and I find my eyelids growing heavy. I don't normally sleep at night; my

resting hours come after sunrise. It's a bit of a job require-
ment. But I haven't closed my eyes in several days, my ex-
cursions with Viola consuming my usual naptime.

It's a good thing I'm a tireless guardian. An *indefati-
gable* sentry. Those are fancy ways to say I never sleep on
the job.

So as you might imagine, I'm a bit flustered when I'm
awoken several hours later by a strange clatter in Hetty's
room. I leap to my feet—or canine paws, actually.

Fortunately, the noise is just the old radiator. It rattles
like mice in a metal exercise wheel, then hisses a puff of
steam from its release valve.

Hetty is still in her bed, although her covers are rum-
pled in an untidy pile. My eyes dart around the room and
I see that her bedroom door is slightly ajar. It seems she's
been up and about and I slept right through it.

My paws hit the floor silently and I wedge my nose
into the crack of the door, easing it open just wide enough
to squeeze through. As a precaution, I creep down the hall
to investigate what she's been up to, expecting to find the
remains of a late-night snack or some other harmless evidence of her nocturnal wandering. Instead, I find something more troubling.

The apartment door is open, the dead bolt loose. Just
like the other night when I discovered the Netherkin in the

elevator. I quickly glance around the kitchen, but there's no one else here. I peek past the door and find the building's hallway empty too. Maybe the lock's broken. Mamita should really have a word with the superintendent. Then again, is it possible Hetty opened it herself? Whatever the reason, I nudge it shut with my snout and head back down the hall.

When I'm halfway to the bedroom, my body tenses in alarm. The sensation of claws on a chalkboard crawls up my spine. I break into a run.

I burst inside. Hetty is still asleep, but she's tossing and turning. Her bare feet have kicked off the blanket and sheets. The room seems empty, but it's alive—dancing with a dangerous energy. I hear an unfamiliar sound. Not the radiator this time—it's the electric noise machine. The steady scratch of its tone has gone choppy. Somewhere, hidden within the static of the white noise, is a low bass throb. Just a hint of a voice. Its words muffled and distorted.

Another foreign sound draws my attention. Jingling. The wind chime is moving, its colorful shards clicking against one another as if blown by an invisible breeze. But the window remains tightly shut.

Then I see it. A dark silhouette peering in the window. I can't make out many details through the shadows, but its face is pressed between both hands on the dirty glass. It has emaciated palms and long fingers that seem almost skeletal, all covered in patchy fur.

One long ear stands up from its head, the other crooked and drooping.

In the gleam of passing headlights, I see two red eyes and a mouthful of oversized, over*eager* teeth.

The Black Rabbit.

I flash into my more familiar wisp form of a boy as I tear across the bedroom. If I'm in for a fight, I want to be comfortable. But as I reach the window, the uninvited visitor pushes back from the glass. The Black Rabbit hesitates for a moment, then hops down the rungs of the fire escape's ladder with a padding of thick paws.

I crane my neck to see where he's gone. Every instinct screams for me to chase him, hunt him down and demand an explanation. But Hetty has caught my attention. She's tossing and turning, as if fighting a fever. I can't risk leaving her alone. What if another prowler is waiting for me to do exactly that?

Don't worry, Hetty, I'm still here.

I study the noise machine. Its static tone is even and soothing once again, the little green button on its face glowing harmlessly. If I didn't know better, I might think my ears had betrayed me. But I'm not so easily fooled.

I carefully pull Hetty's blanket back up over her and slump down in the cushy yellow chair next to Mr. Jum-Jums.

"Keep your eyes peeled, would you, please?" I tell his unblinking orange face. "I could really use some help here."

He's of no use, of course. But this time, I don't doze off again.

I've resumed my cuddly canine form by the time morning comes. Hetty has overslept and her eyes are at half-mast as she rushes to get ready for school. Her mother needs to leave before her in order to get Tomás to day care and make it to work on time herself, and she heaps Hetty with praise for sleeping through the night as she scrambles to collect her jacket and purse. She reminds Hetty to pack a bag when she gets home from school. Apparently, Mamita is working a double shift and Hetty and Tomás will be spending the night with a relative in the suburbs.

As soon as her mother and brother are safely on their way, Hetty rushes back to her bedroom with great excitement. She pulls her purple journal from the desk drawer, jumps cross-legged into the chair, and begins scribbling inside.

"Did you see him, Clover?" she asks excitedly without looking up from the page. "He came again last night."

I cock my head warily.

"He asked if I could open the door so he could come inside and talk."

I cringe. Yeah, Hetty, that's a *really* bad idea. Never take instructions from voices that whisper in the dark.

"He didn't, though," she says with a hint of disappointment. "It's like he got distracted by something and left without saying goodbye."

Yes, well, you can thank me for that later.

"You're looking at me like I'm crazy, Clover, but I think it must be my father. I mean, it doesn't really look like him—he's just sort of a scratchy silhouette—but who else could it be?"

Hetty stops scribbling and looks down at her work. She frowns.

"It's not very good—I mean, it's just a quick sketch." She hesitates, self-conscious. "Here, do you want to see him?"

Hetty turns the journal around and spreads the pages. I creep over for a better look, expecting to find a drawing of a hideous, oversized jackrabbit. But she surprises me, and I can't stifle a low growl.

"I told you it's just a quick sketch. I can do better," she

explains, as if hoping for my approval. "Come on, it's not that bad."

Yes, Hetty. I'm afraid it is.

On the page, a familiar figure looms from Hetty's rough pencil sketch. He's long and lanky, in oversized clothes stretched by his spindly limbs. His head is cocked to the side as if balanced on a spineless neck, and a blank face stares at me with hollow black eye sockets. He has no hair, but his skull is topped with the five points of an ill-fitting crown.

It's an unmistakable portrait of the Boneless King.

16

BETRAYED

Fortunately, Hetty realizes that it's not a great idea to keep a stray animal locked in her apartment all day. On her way to school, she sneaks me into the courtyard and begs me to stay hidden until she returns home. This would seem to be an impossible task for a real dog, but I dutifully hide myself under a stone bench until she leaves. Once she's gone, I'm relieved to shed my disguise and assume my usual wisp form. I drop myself onto the bench and bury my face in my palms.

I'm exhausted and would like nothing more than to return to my roof for some much-needed sleep. But I can't afford to rest. My Domain—and my wards—are under siege. And I don't know why.

The Boneless King has proven himself to be a formidable foe. Not only can he summon Netherkin, but he can also visit the sleeping minds of the living. Clearly he's not alive, and yet he doesn't *feel* like the rest of the dead. I don't believe for one minute that the Boneless King is Hetty's father, and yet he's cunning enough to persuade her otherwise. But *why*? And why, if he's so determined to get to her, does he need an invitation? A powerful creature of the night who can command the dead but can't enter the dwelling of the living—what kind of strange abomination is he?

What was that you were just thinking? Well, *stop* it. I'm nothing like that gum-legged ghoul.

The puzzling questions send my gut churning. Either that, or the cat food's finally catching up with me. What starts as a small burning ember in my stomach quickly grows into a full-blown inferno. I pull my hood over my head and wrap my arms around my body as if that might smother the fire. I'm doubled over in discomfort when I hear Viola's voice.

"Goyle," she calls.

I glance around the courtyard, but I'm still alone.

"Goyle? Are you here?" she calls more loudly.

Viola's voice comes from the alleyway on the other side of the garden wall.

I push myself up and head for the back gate. "I'm in the courtyard," I say.

I crack open the gate and trudge back to my seat on the bench. Viola peeks through hesitantly, then steps inside.

"Goyle, what happened?" She approaches carefully, then eases herself down alongside me. She sets her violin case between us, but I'm too pained to give it my usual attention.

"Cat food," I groan. "Hetty made me eat a big bowl of it."

Viola scrunches her face and scratches her wool cap. I haven't seen her in two days. She still wears the same torn leggings, boots, and old pea coat. Her face is even paler than before. Her eyes probe me.

"She wouldn't take no for an answer," I explain. Viola continues to look at me blankly.

"I didn't *like* it or anything," I quickly fib. "It was awful—"

"Goyle," Viola interrupts, "I'm not asking what you had for dinner."

I sigh. Nobody ever appreciates the sacrifices I make.

"Where have you been?" she asks. "I tried to find you on the roof last night. Do you know how long I talked to your shell before I realized you weren't just giving me the silent treatment?"

"I stayed in the apartment."

Her eyes brighten. "What did you find?"

"Well, Hetty's got some strange stuffed animals and the floor under her bed could use a good dusting. . . ."

Viola isn't amused.

"But, more to your point," I say, "some visitors have been stopping by after dark. And she's not exactly discouraging them."

Viola raises an eyebrow in alarm.

"Our friend from the subway tunnels and the cemetery? The Black Rabbit? I'm pretty sure I spotted him outside her window."

"What do you mean she's not discouraging them?" Viola asks.

"Well, she seems to think that her dead father is communicating with her while she sleeps. He's been asking her to let him come inside the apartment. She writes all this down in a journal she keeps locked away in a drawer." I narrow my eyes. "I don't like that journal one bit. It stinks of danger. At first I thought it was the physical book itself, but now I know it's her own thoughts that are a threat. She's being misled."

Viola shakes her head in disbelief. "She thinks the Black Rabbit is her *father*?"

"No, not him," I say. "The Boneless King. He's been whispering to Hetty in her dreams, even though he's not physically there." I hold Viola's eyes. "Netherkin can't do that—not even Shadow Men. Anything that can is far more sinister."

"You're sure it was the Boneless King?" she asks quietly.

I nod. "Viola drew a picture in her journal. There's no mistaking him."

I pause, poking my fingers around my stomach. It feels like there's something swimming in there. Viola's silent. When I look up, her face has fallen. It's somewhere far away.

"Viola?"

She snaps out of it. "Sorry, I was just thinking."

I may have shared too much. I think I've frightened her.

"You don't need to worry about Hetty," I say, trying to reassure her. "I've got this under control. This is what I do," I add confidently. Although, in truth, I'm plagued by a foreign sensation I can't seem to shake. Doubt? Is that what's swishing around in my gut?

"I know you do," Viola says. "It's not that. It's just . . . I'm a little preoccupied today."

I notice Viola's fingers. They twitch involuntarily,

nervously stroking and twisting the crimson streak in her pigtail.

"I'm already late for rehearsal," she adds.

I raise my scarred eyebrow. "For the concert?"

She steadies her hands and pushes herself to her feet. "Yes . . . the concert."

I examine her violin case. She grabs it before I'm tempted to put a hand on it myself. "Sorry, I have to run."

"Okay, if you really have to go," I say.

"I'll come check on you again soon," she says as she hurries toward the open gate. I notice a waver in her voice. Something's not right.

"I'll be waiting," I say. "Have a good rehearsal."

I see Viola steal a glance at me as she pauses, and I offer her a wave goodbye. She flicks a hand in reply, then disappears into the alley.

I give her another moment, then spring to my feet and rush after her.

I hurry along between feet and ankles, resisting the urge to bury my nose in every crack along the sidewalk and investigate the tantalizing smells.

I've assumed the wisp form of a dog again. It's not a

bad way to get around and helps me keep a low profile. Viola is less likely to spot me.

No, I'm not *spying*, just following her. There's a difference—sort of.

The important part is that I'm worried about her. It's a strange thing to admit. Viola's not my ward and I've known her less than a week, but she is my friend. I've never had a human friend before, but with the Twins gone she's the only one I've got. Friends stick together, right? She said so herself. And she's definitely gone out of her way to help me with my wards. Sometimes, just having someone to talk to can make all the difference. Besides, it's not lost on me that my words deeply troubled her this morning. Or that she hasn't changed her clothes in days. Or that her parents have no problem with her coming and going at all hours of the day and night. I'm beginning to wonder if Viola has anyone else who cares about her at all.

Fortunately, in a city full of practice-adults, the music students are easy to spot. They roam the streets with steaming cups of coffee, black instrument cases slung over their shoulders or pulled behind them on wheels. Their hair is more likely to be dyed in shades of blue, green, and other colors that don't grow naturally. Their skin tones reflect backgrounds that are far-flung and diverse. Right now, the sidewalk in front of the Conservatory is bustling as they head inside for class and rehearsals.

Viola is by far the shortest and youngest of the bunch. I've kept a healthy distance, but I can see that she doesn't speak to any of the other students who busily chat in small groups as they walk. I wonder if it's hard for her to make friends with this older crowd. I know what it's like to be an outsider. I suddenly feel guilty about intruding on a part of her life she's seemed reluctant to share.

Still, my guilt turns to anticipation as the young musicians hurry inside. Since I'm here anyway, maybe I'll slip in for a quick listen. I'm eager to hear Viola—she must be a rare talent to be admitted among these more experienced peers. But I'm surprised to see her break away from the pack and continue down the street. I think she might stop at a corner convenience store, but she walks right past that too, leaving the Conservatory far behind. She's walking purposefully, as if it was never her destination at all.

I pick up my pace to match her own as she hurries across a busy intersection, but I'm stopped midstride by a familiar sensation. I turn quickly and spot a rattling newspaper box that appears to shudder with the breeze. Inside, a small white imp the size of a squirrel is devouring copies of the Sunday *Herald*.

Nuisance. I've no time for you right now.

I turn my attention back to Viola only to find that I've lost sight of her.

Bricks and mortar!

She's disappeared into the bowels of the city.

I glower through the little glass window of the newspaper box. The imp looks up, a mouthful of the sports pages dangling from his teeth. Realizing I'm no mere dog, his bloodshot eyes widen in terror.

It's your lucky day, imp. I've got no stomach for you. At this moment, there's only one thing on my mind.

Viola lied to me.

17

OLD CROAK'S

My keen nose sniffs the air for clues. I double back and retrace my steps to where I last saw Viola. I hop a curb. Hurdle a storm drain. And then, to my relief, I spot her. Her wool cap is low on her head, her eyes glued down on the sidewalk as she hurries away from the neighborhood.

This time I have no intention of losing her. She glances over her shoulder once or twice, but I'm too good at this. A century of sneaking up on imps has made me a skilled tracker. I keep a healthy distance between us.

I'm not sure what any of this means. Is Viola lying about rehearsal or did she just decide to skip it? Maybe this has all just become a bit too much for her. The world of Grotesques and Netherkin and Boneless Kings would be enough to send the bravest children running home for the security of their beds.

Her path takes us through the theater district and out the other side. She's making an erratic, circular loop, then doubling back, as if aware that someone could be following her. Of course, I *am* following her, but I don't think it's me she's worried about. Then again, maybe I shouldn't try to guess *what* Viola is thinking. It occurs to me that we've spent plenty of time talking about me and my wards these past few days, but I hardly know any more about Viola than I did the first night we met.

The grand old theaters are all empty on a weekday, and the nearby restaurants currently draw all the crowds. Viola finally stops at the brick and limestone façade of a six-story building that looks as old as me. I'm unfamiliar with it—my travels don't bring me this way often. But I have a vague recollection that they once sold pianos here.

The street-level storefront is boarded up and abandoned. A FOR LEASE sign is nailed to the plywood, but I doubt there'll be any takers. The bricks are charred. The fabric awning is gone and only a thin metal frame remains. Over the door, engraved letters in the limestone are blackened but still legible.

OLD CROAK'S STONE
WORK AND ENGRAVING

Viola looks up and down the street one last time. When there's a break in pedestrian traffic, she slips through a thin gap in the plywood sheets. I give her a few seconds, then follow close behind.

The shop hasn't just been burned—it's obliterated. Black and scorched from floor to ceiling; if there were ever walls or furnishings, they've been reduced to piles of ash. I might as well be standing inside a cast-iron stove after a long winter.

I feel another pang of discomfort in my stomach. If this bleak tomb is where Viola lives, she's in far worse shape than I imagined.

"Viola," I whisper, although there's no need to lower my voice. She's the only one who can hear me anyway.

"Viola," I call more loudly, but there's no reply.

I check the floor for her footprints, but I can't make any sense of the patterns in the soot. Yes, I know I said I was an expert tracker, but imps don't leave footprints—I don't have a lot of practice in this area.

I do find the remains of some stacked granite slabs half buried in the debris. They pop up in piles like ancient stalagmites. Upon closer inspection, I see that they are naked headstones waiting to be carved and engraved. It makes sense. This *was* an engraver's shop. Given the number of stones, he must have been a busy one.

I look closer. The granite headstones are actually scorched. As the owner of a granite shell myself, I can tell you that stone doesn't burn easily. That tells *me* how hot the blaze must have been.

I creep toward the back of the shop, but Viola is nowhere to be found. I spot an old freight elevator. You already know my disdain for elevators, but this one is out of order anyway. I know this because its door has been torn free and lies on its side, the interior gears and buttons already picked clean by looters. But it means there's another floor here and gives me a hint as to where Viola may have gone. Another moment and I find a small doorway and a narrow flight of stairs descending into some sort of basement.

The stairway is steep and narrow, built in a time when the average person didn't take up so much space. It smells of mold and baked-in smoke, but the stairs themselves seem structurally sound. They continue for what must be several stories, and I'm surprised that they lead much deeper than what would normally be basement level.

Finally, I reach the end. And a heavy steel door.

Thinking it might be locked, I give it a shove with all my strength. But it just eases open, as if it's been expecting me. I step through.

"Bricks," I whisper in awe.

A cavernous subterranean theater looms all around me.

The stucco walls and tall Corinthian pillars are crumbling and pockmarked. The balconies are deserted. Most of the seats have been removed. In their place, the floor is littered with the smashed remains of granite statues.

The wreckage is everywhere.

"You found me, Goyle," a small voice says.

I turn quickly at the sound. It's coming from a stage that isn't home to instruments or music stands, but is instead cluttered with stacks of shipping crates and boxes covered with dusty tarps. Viola sits on one of the crates, her violin case in her lap.

"Viola," I say, still casting my eyes around. "What *is* this place?"

"It used to be a concert hall," she says. "Once the finest in the city."

Viola glances up at the balconies and the vaulted ceiling

high above us. The paint is now peeling and its peak is crisscrossed with a maze of corroded sprinkler pipes.

"The acoustics are still perfect," she says, and cups a hand to her ear. "Listen. No street noise. We're deeper than the subway tunnels."

With my keen hearing, I can tell what she means. We're insulated from the outside world down here. Viola's voice carries perfectly in this haunting place.

"There was a huge fire at a nightclub," she says. "Back in the thirties or forties, I think. It was so bad the city changed all the fire codes. Unfortunately, the theater couldn't meet them. It had to be shut down and never re-opened."

I remember that fire. Over four hundred souls lost—tragically and unexpectedly. I actually took pity on them—even the ones who wandered the city for years before finally moving on to what's Next.

"For a while, the building's owner would let famous musicians come down here to record their music," Viola continues. "The hidden concert hall became a bit of a legend—whispered among visiting orchestras. But somewhere along the way, the owners stopped allowing visitors altogether."

Viola glances around at the rusting ironwork, crumbling pillars, and scattered debris.

"Safety concerns," she adds.

I purse my lips and catch her eyes. "Do you ... live down here?"

She's quiet for a moment. "This is where I stay. For now."

I drop my eyes to the debris on the floor, then look up again. "Why here? Don't you have a family?"

She shakes her head. Ever so slightly.

"You're not a music student, are you?"

Another shake of her head.

"Why didn't you tell me?" I ask. "Why did you lie?" To my surprise, I find myself more hurt than angry.

Viola's response comes slowly. "I didn't want you to think of me differently than everybody else."

With all the terrible things humans do to one another, it's strange that they find themselves ashamed of things beyond their control.

"I had a foster family," she says. "They ... weren't kind."

She doesn't need to explain. I've been around long enough to see how cruel some families—foster or otherwise—can be.

"When I couldn't take it anymore, I left. I had nowhere to go for a while. Then I met the owner of the shop upstairs. Samuel. He went home to his family each night but let me stay down here in exchange for sweeping floors, running errands. I don't think he really needed the help, but he wanted to give me somewhere to stay."

I remember a time when no one paid much attention to runaways. Things are different now.

"He could have gotten into a lot of trouble," I point out. "You can't just take in strange children off the street and keep them like lost pets."

She shrugs. "He was kind. And more concerned about helping me than getting into trouble."

"*Was?*" I repeat.

Viola nods. "There was a fire—in the shop. I'm sure you noticed." She pauses. "He was working inside at the time." Her lip starts to tremble but she pinches it with her teeth.

"He wasn't able to get out?" I ask.

Viola sags on the empty crate. "The fire came on so suddenly. It was late at night; the streets were deserted—nobody else was here at the time. Nobody who could help."

She hangs her head.

I shift from foot to foot. I'm not good with this sort of thing. I don't know what to say.

"I wish I could have done something," she says finally.

I know how she feels. I'm thinking of my ward—that little boy long ago. Of Wallace and Winnie. I wasn't there for them either. My eyes dance over the broken granite pieces on the floor.

"It's not your fault," I mutter.

I notice a chunk of granite tooth. A long, sharp canine.

"You can't blame yourself," I say.

I see the remains of a stone arm, broken off from the elbow down. The chipped hand has talons instead of fingers.

"You couldn't have—" I start, then stop.

I spot a disembodied tail.

I turn back abruptly to Viola. Suddenly, all my senses are charged. How did I not notice this right away?

"Viola, I'm going to ask again," I say, my tone darkening. "What *is* this place?"

All around us, we are surrounded by destroyed Grotesques.

18

THE BONE MASON

I find a clawed foot. Then a broken wing.

A cracked head rests on its ear, its lifeless eyes staring out at the rubble as if searching for its body.

I'm sick to my stomach—and it's not from last night's dinner.

"Did *you* do this?" I demand in disbelief. "Did *he*?"

"Of course not," Viola replies hotly. "Samuel *created* Grotesques, he didn't destroy them."

I step heavily toward her. Viola tenses and recoils. I still seem to frighten her, even without trying.

"Stop speaking in riddles, Viola."

"Samuel was a Bone Mason, Goyle. The last one left in the city. This was his workshop."

"A *Bone Mason*?"

"Yes." Viola searches for some understanding in my face but must recognize my blank expression. Her own eyes turn uncertain. "You don't know?" she asks.

"Know *what*?"

"Who made you."

"My Maker made me," I say quickly.

She blinks, and confusion washes over her. "I always just assumed you knew. . . ."

Suddenly I feel defensive, put on the spot. "I don't know *exactly* who he was," I say. "I never met him or anything like that."

Viola steadies her expression and fixes her gaze on me. "Your Maker was a Mason," she says quietly. "Just like the one who worked here."

I'm stunned by the insult. Then angry. I glance around at this place, remembering the granite slabs and broken tools in the burned-out shop above us.

"I'm not some *tombstone*, Viola," I say bitterly. "Do I look like an ornament to you? Can a hitching post do the things I do?"

"Of course not," she says, jumping to her feet. "Yes, Samuel engraved headstones and carved fountains when he needed to pay the rent, but *this* was his real craft." She waves her arms at the broken bodies around us. "He was a *Bone* Mason. He learned those skills from his father. And his father's father before him. In fact, go back one more father . . ." Viola looks at the floor, then back at me. "And that was *your* very own Maker."

I study Viola carefully. She's lied to me once already, but there's nothing in her face that leads me to believe she's doing so again. Still, I don't like this feeling that she knows more about me than I know myself. Not one bit. It's like stumbling alone through a dark room, then turning on a light and realizing someone's been next to you watching the whole time.

I eye her suspiciously. "Tell me more about Bone Masons."

"I wish I could. They've been around for hundreds—maybe thousands—of years, but the practice of Bone Masonry is a mystery. Its secrets are only revealed to other Masons after decades of apprenticeship."

"Then it sounds to me like you don't know much of anything at all," I say gruffly.

"You're right," Viola says, and for a moment I'm relieved. Then, to my surprise, slightly disappointed.

"But there are two things I *do* know," she continues, pacing through the rubble as she talks. "First, every Grotesque is sculpted with a human bone embedded in its shell. It's a bone taken from someone recently deceased—usually a child. They're the souls most likely to be pure of heart. It's called the Root. The Root brings you life." Viola stops her pacing. "Or at least your version of it."

"So my Maker was a grave robber?" I say in disgust and disbelief. "Bone Masons go around digging up children's bodies and stealing their bones? They sound worse than Netherkin."

Viola shakes her head. "No, it's not like that. That's where the second part comes in. With each Root, there's also a Remnant—some important artifact from that person's life. It's given voluntarily by the donor's loved ones, then preserved by the Bone Mason himself. Passed down to his successors. The Remnant is what binds you here. It's what keeps you from moving on."

My jaw tightens. "It keeps us prisoner?"

"Don't think of it that way," she says. "Think of all the good you do. All the wards you protect. Now imagine a grieving family that's lost a child. It's an opportunity for them to give new purpose to a life cut far too short."

This all sounds outlandish. Impossible to believe. Then again, if you told me a week ago that I'd be spending my days gabbing with a homeless girl who plays an imaginary violin, I'd have said you had mortar between your ears. I look down at my wisp form. Clearly no bone resides in me at the moment, but . . . back on the roof . . . deep within my stone body? Can I be so certain? What Root lies within the very shell I've called home for so long? What Remnant binds *me* to this place? If what Viola says is true, *what* exactly am I?

"You're telling me I'm just some child?" I say.

Viola offers a tight smile. "Part of you *was* a child." She holds her thumb and forefinger apart. "Just a tiny bit. Now you're a Grotesque. And what *that* means, well, I think only you get to say."

I cast my arms at the fragments of broken Grotesques strewn around our feet. "And these," I say. "They were all once children too?"

"No, these were just the shells. Works in progress. They have no Roots or Remnants. Samuel was just preparing them, in case"—her eyes drift away—"they were ever needed."

"So if Samuel didn't destroy them, and you didn't, then who?"

Viola's eyes darken.

"Netherkin," she says coldly. "Sent by the Boneless King."

If I had blood, it would run cold.

"Two strange men came knocking after hours, just

before the fire," she continues. "Samuel mistook them for men, anyway. Somehow they convinced him to let them inside, and they caught Samuel by surprise."

My lips curl with contempt. Shadow Men—the most devious of all Netherkin. And masters of disguise.

"They killed the last Bone Mason in the city, Goyle." Viola crosses her arms tightly as if battling a chill, glancing over the crumbled stones around us. "And made sure there could be no more Grotesques."

So Viola had heard of the Boneless King even before I did. Again, I have the sickening feeling that I've been stumbling through the dark. It's not my fault. It's not like our Makers hand us a guidebook—or even bother to introduce themselves. You just sort of open your eyes one day and there you are on the roof. The rest you're left to make sense of on your own.

But something tells me Viola knows even more. I fight my urge to be angry at her and push forward with questions, determined to find out exactly what.

"And what kind of monster is the Boneless King, Viola?" I ask. "He's not like any Netherkin I've ever known."

"His name is—well, it *was*—Hannibal Craven the Younger. He was a Bone Mason of modest ability. Not to be confused with his father, Hannibal Craven the Elder, a Mason of much greater skill and notoriety."

"You're not painting a very rosy picture of these people," I grumble.

"It gets worse," Viola says. "Craven the Younger went mad. He became obsessed with making a name for himself outside of his father's shadow. He wanted to ensure his own immortality—*literally*. Craven was convinced that if he could bring stone to life using the bones of the dead, he should be able to use those same techniques to give himself eternal life."

"He wanted to make himself into a Grotesque?"

Viola nods.

I roll my eyes. "I suppose the grass is always greener. . . ."

I wonder for a moment what it must be like to be human; to have a family, or to dream, or to sit and simply touch the hand of someone like Viola. But if there is the Root of a child somewhere inside me, does that mean I've already had all those things? I quickly come to my senses and shake off the inconvenient notion before I miss any more of Viola's story.

"Craven couldn't wait until he was dead to try it, of course," Viola is saying. "And he couldn't find another Bone Mason to help him—it goes against every code of their order. So he performed the procedure himself. He summoned his longtime apprentice to help him—a failed stage performer called the Magician. Together, they removed Craven's tibia from his leg."

Viola runs a finger from her knee to her ankle. "That's the shinbone right here."

"He let some huckster magician do that? He *was* mad."

"The Magician was also the local butcher—which I suppose gave him some experience in ... deboning." She shudders at the thought. "Craven decided that being hobbled was a fair trade for everlasting life."

"I'm going to guess things didn't go as planned."

"No. In fact, it went horribly wrong. Exactly what happened next is unknown, but it's been said that when they finished setting the stone and reciting the final incantations, Craven's Grotesque exploded on its pedestal in a rain of granite—along with every other bone in the insane Bone Mason's body. The pain was so excruciating it killed him on the spot. Terrified that he'd be charged with murder, the Magician hid Craven's body, burying him in a shallow grave."

"So *that's* what friends are for," I say.

"But Craven wasn't dead. Not exactly. Several weeks later he dug himself from the earth, emerging as a disoriented, boneless mass of skin neither living nor dead. The first thing he did was track down his old friend the

Magician. The Bone Masons know this because the local constable found the Magician in his butcher's shop dressed in his stage tailcoat, his black top hat resting on the counter. The Magician himself was hanging upside down next to a rack of lamb."

"And that's how the Boneless King was born," I say.

Viola nods. "He's wandered the earth ever since in a state of limbo. Neither man nor Grotesque, he uses his influence on the dead to try to lay claim on the world of the living—a world he lost the right to be part of long ago."

It explains why I struggled to recognize the Boneless King for what he was the first night we met. He's no Netherkin, nor is he any mortal man. But part Grotesque? It seems impossible. And yet, could that be why he can't enter Hetty's apartment? Could he be bound by the same unwritten rules as me?

"If his shinbone's his Root, what's his Remnant?" I ask.

"No one knows. And no one knows where it's hidden. Otherwise the Bone Masons would have retrieved it and cut his ties to this world once and for all. Instead, all they can do is weaken him each time he emerges, beating him back into the ground."

I recall that battle with the army of Netherkin so long ago. The unseasonable snowstorm and oppressive energy in the skies overhead. The deafening hum of static.

It's been a hundred years, but it's all repeating itself. The Boneless King's war has already started again—I've just been too dense to accept it.

"After he's been weakened and beaten into the ground—what happens then?" I say.

"He lies dormant. Sometimes for decades. But the Boneless King is like a weed. Cutting him down just seems to make him grow back even stronger. When he's ready, he creeps to the surface to choke the life out of all he touches."

"Why here? And why now?"

Viola shrugs. "Hannibal Craven lived here for some time during his youth. That might have something to do with it. But again, think of a weed. As the Boneless King, he now finds a weak spot—a crack in the sidewalk—to push through while he's still frail."

"For a long time, it was just me and the Twins here," I say, blinking slowly. "And now . . . it's even weaker still."

Viola's voice grows more desperate. "The Boneless King may start small, but with no Grotesques or Bone Masons to resist him, his army will grow quickly, until eventually there'll be no way to stop him."

I drop myself down onto a tarped crate. I've always thought of myself as a clever Grotesque. There's not much I can't get my mind around with enough time to sit and ponder. But at the moment, my head is spinning. I feel like I've toppled from my roof and landed tail up.

I narrow a suspicious eye under my hood.

"Viola, if you only swept floors and ran errands, how can you possibly know all this?"

"I thought you might ask that," she says. "I'll show you. Can you please move?"

"What?"

She gestures to my wobbly seat. "I'll show you how I know, but you're sitting on my answer."

I rise to my feet and she takes hold of the tarp that covers the old storage crate. But when she flings the canvas off with a flutter of dust, I discover that it's not a crate at all. Instead, I see a stack of leather-bound workbooks. Hundreds of them.

"I found these tucked under the stage in some boxes," Viola says. "Samuel's journals. They must not have meant anything to the Boneless King. That, or he never found them."

Viola keeps talking, but I'm intently studying the well-worn covers.

"I wanted you to follow me here, Goyle," she is saying. "If I'd told you all this on your roof you'd never have believed me. But here, where you can see it all with your own eyes, I hope you realize I'm telling the truth."

I carefully run my fingers over the covers. Most are in shades of brown and black, but some are dyed different colors. Dark green. Scarlet. Purple. I've seen a journal like these before.

Locked away in Hetty's drawer.

"Goyle," Viola says, then hesitates. "There's another part of this I need to tell you."

But she doesn't have to. I'm not some vacant-eyed water fountain.

Hetty wants to believe that the Boneless King is her father—back from the dead to reunite with her while she sleeps. She has no way of knowing who or what her night-time visitor really is. But the Boneless King, I'm now certain, knows *exactly* who Hetty's father was. He murdered him in this very spot.

"Samuel was Hetty's father," I declare between gritted teeth.

Whatever was churning in my gut is now burning.

"Yes," Viola confirms. "And there's one more thing—" she whispers hesitantly, but I cut her off.

"I've heard enough for now, Viola."

She can't see the fury building under my hood, which is probably for the best.

"Come with me," I say. "I have something I need to show *you*."

19

UNDER THE DRAGON

We sit on the curb across from the abandoned chapel, puddles from the morning's scattered rain pooling at our feet. The spray from passing traffic keeps showering the street performer on the chapel steps, until he finally packs up his guitar and empty hat and sulks away.

My eyes remain on the Twins, perched on the eaves overhead. Of course, they're not the Twins anymore. Wallace's once-keen eyes have gone dull; Winnie's talkative lips remain frozen in permanent silence.

"Who were they?" Viola asks.

"Winnie and Wallace," I say. "They were my friends.

Family, really. I've known them since ... well, for as long as I can remember. We've been through everything together—perched shoulder to shoulder during our darkest times."

Viola fidgets with the violin case she's rested upright between her knees. "Which was which?" she asks.

"Winnie's the better-looking one," I say.

Viola squints back and forth at their grimacing faces.

"The one on the right," I clarify.

"Oh, of course," she says. Then, after a moment, "What happened to them?"

"They were destroyed—incinerated. I don't know exactly what happened, I wasn't there. I was supposed to meet them but I was late. As always. By the time I arrived, all that was left was scorched brick." I turn to look at Viola. "Just like the inside of Samuel's shop."

Viola lowers her eyes and fiddles with the handle of her case.

"I crossed paths with the Boneless King that night on my way to meet them. I didn't know who or what he was at the time, but I should have paid closer attention." I feel myself begin to simmer. "He's been here before, Viola. A long time ago. We just didn't have a name or face for him. Back then, it got ... pretty bad. I lost—" I try to swallow back my words.

"Lost what?"

"I lost one of my—"

The front doors of the chapel open unexpectedly, and I see two uniformed officers escorting a bewildered, unshaven man down the steps. It's the squatter who's lived peacefully in the basement of the Twins' Domain for as long as I can remember. He's never bothered anyone.

This is what becomes of our wards once we're gone.

My insides come to a full boil.

"Goyle, I have something else I need to tell you," Viola whispers, but I barely hear her.

"The Boneless King and his Netherkin are hunting Bone Masons and Grotesques," I spit. "They destroyed Hetty's father. I have no doubt who's responsible for taking the Twins. And now they're after Hetty. *My* ward."

"I think you're right, Goyle," Viola says. "But listen to me, I think I can help. I just need to—"

"I'll crush him," I snap. "I won't rest until every last Netherkin in this city is in my gullet."

Viola goes silent. She runs her fingers up and down the crimson streak in her pigtail and adjusts her cap low over her eyes. When she speaks again, her voice is measured.

"Goyle, you can't possibly track down every Netherkin by yourself," she's saying. "And you don't need to. It's the Boneless King you have to worry about."

"They're one and the same," I say angrily. "They do his bidding. And if he's going to hide while they do all the dirty work, they'll pay the price until I find one to help me root him out."

"How are you going to do that?" Viola implores. "I don't get the impression any Netherkin are going to stick around long enough to introduce you."

"Probably not," I say, glowering. "Except for one."

Viola's knuckles go white on the handle of her violin case.

"And I've got a bone or two to pick with him."

By day, without the benefit of music and talkative crowds, the Copper Dragon is just an old, dark restaurant smelling of last night's spilled drinks and this afternoon's greasy sandwiches. There's nobody outside to check IDs at the door.

I glance up at the placard. The useless copper dragon eyes us sleepily. I'm not worried about stepping on any toes—or claws.

My search for answers probably should have brought me here first. But truth be told, I couldn't bring myself to return. I didn't want to see the Twins this way again, remember them as two scorched streaks on the side of a wall. I still won't. My destination is inside.

"Stay here, Viola," I say.

"Why?"

"It's a tavern. No place for children."

"It's the middle of the day," she protests.

"Can you just take my advice?" I ask wearily. "I promise to tell you everything as soon as I'm done."

She stares at me, unrelenting. But I spend my days as a statue—there's no way she's going to win this contest.

I stand my ground until she finally takes a reluctant seat on the curb; then I push through the front door. I stomp past the waitresses as they clear tables and ready for their evening shifts. I'm not subtle, but they can't see me anyway. They may catch a chill as I pass but nothing more. The place is lifeless and dreary, the air stale. I round the corner and reach an old, seldom-used door, but stop in my tracks.

"Viola!" I gasp. "What are you doing in here?" I do a double take to the front of the tavern, and glance around at the employees. Fortunately, they're all busy with their tasks. "How did you get in here?"

"Kitchen door was open," she says, thrusting her thumb behind her. "I never actually agreed to stay outside," she says quickly, before I can protest. "You just *assumed*."

I grumble. I don't have the stomach for a debate.

"Fine. But please—keep your distance and let me do the talking. Onesimus can be shifty."

"Onesimus?"

"The Netherkin in the basement. He can't move much anymore—that is, if he's there at all. But he can still be dangerous if you get too close."

The Copper Dragon's basement is really just a crawl space, its earthen floor littered with forgotten casks and discarded supplies. Even in my wisp form of a boy, I still need to duck my head to navigate it. Like the lair of a giant spider, it's covered in a tapestry of gray cobwebs. They catch a ray of dim light from a tiny, barred square of glass that looks out on the back alley. The bars are unnecessary; no burglar is likely to venture down here. Even Viola stays at the base of the steps without my asking.

Onesimus is the oldest Netherkin I've ever met. He's been around longer than me, and the details of his demise remain unclear. He once told me he was shot in the back in a duel in the alley behind the Dragon, insisting that his opponent was a dishonorable cheat. I've also heard he was a traitor and a horse thief who got himself hanged in the

Common—he ended up here because a tavern stool was the closest thing he'd ever had to a home. My money's on the latter.

Onesimus is also a compulsive gossip. We made a deal long ago. I spared him in exchange for his promise to provide me with information whenever I called on him. It was once useful to have a gabby Netherkin in my pocket. But he finally went senile and his ramblings became impossible to decipher. I haven't bothered to visit him in years, and wouldn't go to the trouble now if I had any other option. I'm not sure what happens to old Netherkin who linger too long—but I've long since assumed that they eventually just fade away and disappear.

Today I'm relieved to discover that ever-stubborn Onesimus hasn't gone anywhere. I find him sitting cross-legged in a dusty nook, just past the little beam of light. He's more humanoid than most Netherkin—an emaciated, hairless old man, covered in a thin membrane of skin that shimmers like snake scales. It changes colors with his moods. The effect creeps even me out—you know how I feel about snakes.

"Penhallow, my old friend," he rasps. "Is that you?"

Onesimus's skin glimmers pale blue as he unfolds his serpentine limbs, leaning in for a closer look. His head is barely more than a skull. His eyes are only sickly white orbs, and the skin that remains doesn't cover his bare jaw or dull, brittle teeth.

I just stand there with my arms crossed, glowering. Onesimus knows exactly who it is, but he likes to play these little games.

"It *is-s-s* you," he whisper-hisses after a moment. "To what do I owe the pleasure?" He has no lips and frequently licks the spittle that drips down his chin as he talks.

Onesimus is shrewd and perceptive, but my reply surprises even him. I lurch forward and clutch him by the neck.

He tries to shriek and struggle in protest, but he's too weak. For a moment, his form blurs in and out of existence, but I'm not ready to let him go just yet.

"I thought we had an understanding, Onesimus. I thought you knew better."

He can only choke in reply. I loosen my grip and he falls to the dirt floor, kicking up dust. He gasps and his skin shimmers crimson in anger.

When he can speak again, he hisses every curse his decrepit mind can remember.

"I protected you, Onesimus," I say. "My friends would have devoured you the first night we found you here, but I convinced them to let you stay."

"Vile, nasty demons," Onesimus is muttering. His white orbs throb with disdain.

"You remember why I did that, don't you?" I say.

"Monsters. Abominations." He's mumbling now.

"Because I told them you were old, weak, and harmless," I answer for him. He grunts and his skin softens to a peachy red. "All you had to do was stay out of our way. Keep to yourself and rot in this hole."

"That's all I've done!" he spits.

"*And,*" I continue, "keep us informed if trouble was on its way."

Onesimus laps the drool off his chin and furrows what remains of his brow.

"Do you remember *that* part?" I ask.

"I'm very old," he says meekly, his skin pulsing a cool blue again. "My memory often fails me."

I take a menacing step forward. "Do I need to refresh it?"

"No, no. Not necessary," he says. "It's coming back to me now."

Onesimus's skin goes silver and he coils himself back into a cross-legged pile.

"But even with my wits about me," he adds, "I have no idea what's gotten a bee in your bonnet."

"My friends, Onesimus. You know, the ones you were so fond of?"

He shrugs his shoulders unconvincingly.

I glare hard and clench my fists.

"Oh," he says quickly. "You mean the fat mouse and the beady-eyed little wretch?"

I give him a dark nod.

"Yes, well, I haven't seen them in ages."

This time I do lunge, and Onesimus's white orbs go wide as he tries to scamper away.

"Ouch! Stop that, you nasty little ape!" he cries as I grab him by a decaying ear. I give it a hard pinch.

"The last time you would have seen them was a week ago," I point out. "Right here. Before they were incinerated."

"Please let go," he squeals.

"I want you to tell me who did that to them, and where I can find them," I demand. "I'd ask if it was you, but I know better."

"Arrgh!" Onesimus screeches. I realize that as my anger's risen, my grip on his ear has tightened. Suddenly, it's disappeared altogether in a cloud of vapor, and I find my fingers holding nothing at all.

"Now you've done it!" he wails. "I only had two of those, you know!"

"How many Netherkin?" I rage on. "Were they Shadow Men? It would take more than a few to do that to Wallace and Winnie."

Onesimus rubs a palm over his hairless scalp. His skin is a shifting rainbow of ominous colors, reflecting pain, fear, and venom. He looks at me with poison in his milky orbs, but I see them drawn to something over my shoulder. I follow his gaze.

Viola! She's crept from the stairs and is watching from behind a wooden beam. That girl's as stubborn as a fountainhead. I return my glare to Onesimus.

"Netherkin," I repeat. "How many?"

Onesimus just shakes his head.

"Let's try the other ear," I say, and reach for it.

He extends both shimmering palms in front of his face and cowers. "No, I mean not Netherkin!" he cries before I can do more damage. "It was *him.* The one who walks among the living but commands the dead. He's called the Boneless King."

"Yes," I say. "I know the Boneless King sent them."

"Wrong, wrong, wrong," Onesimus insists. "It was the Boneless King himself who met your rodent and the filthy street urchin." Onesimus's skin pulses ominously. "He made quick work of them too. They hardly put up a fight."

The Boneless King alone? Without the aid of Netherkin? If it's true, he's already more powerful than I realized.

"The grubby vermin went first," Onesimus is saying.

He wipes the spittle from his chin with the back of his hand. "Then it was the girl's turn."

I feel my fury rising at the sound of Onesimus's words. I glance back at Viola, who's still watching from behind the beam.

"It was quick, but far from painless," Onesimus adds with a touch of glee.

"Where is he?" I demand.

Onesimus looks up from nursing his injury. He paws the hole left by his missing ear the way a cat cleans its wounds.

"I'm sorry," he says bitterly. "I'm having trouble hearing you. Could you try speaking into my good ear?" He points a shimmering finger to the other side of his head.

I lean forward and growl into his remaining ear. "Tell me where the Boneless King is right now, or I'll grind you into the dust of this basement."

Onesimus's white orbs stare at me hard, and he presses his mouth toward my own ear, resting it against the folds of my hood.

"Tonight the Boneless King rests on his throne. But not for long. He's gathering his army. Calling them from every hollow and crypt in the city. And when he's done . . ." Onesimus's skin flares. "You'll be the one ground into dust—just like your friends."

And with that, Onesimus snaps his brittle teeth down on my own ear.

Fortunately for me, his jaws are weak and his teeth crumble in his mouth. Unfortunately for him, his nip is enough to send me into a rage. This time when I leap and clutch him, my fingers shift into claws. The vest on my back sprouts into wings and my own jaws expand. My teeth are neither weak nor brittle.

I sink them into the feeble old specter. His cries rattle the subterranean walls.

"Where?" I demand.

"I don't know!" He thrashes but can't escape.

"Where?" I repeat, my mouth full. His hand and wrist disappear.

"I don't know! Ask your new friend!"

Behind me, Viola may be calling out my name, but I'm not listening.

"Where?" I say again, and Onesimus's arm disappears up to the elbow.

"I don't know! I wasn't summoned! I'm of no use to him—too old and weak!"

"Then you're of no use to me either," I jeer, and open wide to swallow him whole.

"Goyle, stop!"

I feel something tug at my shoulders and I release him. I swivel around, my eyes blind with fury.

Viola's own face is stricken with terror. She's never seen me like this before.

"*Stop!*" she pleads. "You're torturing him."

I'm stunned. How could she feel empathy for this beast? Can't she understand that this needs to be done?

My glare drills into her in disbelief; then I fix my gaze back on Onesimus. He's dragged himself into his nook in a crumpled, shimmering ball.

"Where?" I say one last time.

"The Spite House," he wheezes. "Up the hill past Christ Church. *That's* where you'll find the Boneless King."

Onesimus's skin flickers crimson as I turn on my heel and stomp out of the crawl space.

He can thank Viola that he's got anything left to flicker at all.

20

THE SPITE HOUSE

I've caught a lucky break tonight. My first in a long time. Hetty and Tomás are sleeping at a relative's house while their mother works late. That means they're away from my Domain, and gives me an opportunity to venture out after dark. It's still a risk, but I think my other wards can spare me. It's Hetty and her family the Boneless King is after.

The energy swirling over Copp's Hill Burying Ground the night we visited makes sense now. That's where the Boneless King has hunkered down. He's biding his time, gathering strength—and an army to do his bidding. Of course, if he's already powerful enough to so easily handle Wallace and Winnie, maybe he's plenty strong already. But I'd like to think Onesimus is exaggerating. I know my friends, and I'm sure they gave that wobbly skin-walker one heck of a fight.

Even so, I can't allow the Boneless King any more time.

Viola insisted on coming with me again. Being the reasonable and forgiving Grotesque that I am, I didn't hold her foolishness in the crawl space against her.

All right, the truth is we got into a knock-down, drag-out argument right in front of the Copper Dragon. I refused to let her come, and Viola pointed out—accurately, to my dismay—that she knew exactly where I was going. She insisted that she'd just follow me anyway.

So here she is by my side as we navigate down a narrow street busy with tourists. They browse menus outside restaurants while locals sip espresso at cafes that have hardly changed in sixty years. Viola doesn't say a word as we weave between leisurely strolling couples—she's hardly said anything at all since our argument. I'm still angry and befuddled by her behavior, but the fact is, I'm relieved she's here. I couldn't have borne the thought of her returning alone to that boneyard of a theater. Not that I'm about to admit it.

"You know, I've met people like you before," I grouse as we go. "*Squids.* Weirdos who can see Netherkin."

"And Grotesques," she mutters.

"Not one of them was right in the head," I say.

"Maybe speaking with invisible *monsters* is enough to make anyone a little crazy," she huffs.

"Or maybe a little too *sympathetic*," I add, a bite in my tone.

She adjusts her wool cap over her eyes and doesn't seem inclined to talk anymore.

We walk past Christ Church, which everyone calls the Old North Church nowadays. The road turns steep as we follow the redbrick path up the hill. When Copp's Hill Burying Ground comes into view, I take the narrow side street nearest where the Black Rabbit fled.

The Spite House is like a spindly, black spider, its impossibly narrow wooden frame lurking in the crevice between two brick neighbors. Its midnight-colored clapboards squeeze upward in the alleyway with the tenacity of a vine. A grown man could almost hug it simply by stretching out his arms. No sane person would have designed a house like this. It could only have been built out of malice or, well, *spite*—probably to ruin the view of a neighbor long ago. A sliver of a front door and four squinty windows face the street—one on each floor, the lowest covered with thin iron bars like bared teeth. A hint of orange candlelight seeps out from behind its sealed shutters.

Just ahead of us, two practice-adults are heading the same way. I pause as they approach the door. One is dressed like some sort of Parisian cleaning woman, stumbling in high-heeled shoes on the cobblestone sidewalk. Her companion looks like a buccaneer who's lost his ship.

"What is this nonsense?" I say. "These two can't be the cleaning service."

Viola rolls her eyes. "Goyle, they're in costume. They're probably headed to a party." She says it as if I'm as clueless as a curb, but at least she's talking again. "Tomorrow's Halloween, remember?"

Actually, I'd completely forgotten. I'm so used to seeing beasties skulk through the night, a few costumes each October hardly faze me.

"At this address?" I ask. "They must be lost."

All Hallows' Eve is not one of my favorite holidays. I don't like strangers popping into my Domain under the best of circumstances, and every year the practice-adults who live with me make a terrible mess of my roof. They're also more inclined to climb on me and take embarrassing pictures.

"Oh, mullions," I say. "Now they're knocking."

The buccaneer raps on the black door of the Spite

House. When there's no immediate response, he tries again. Harder.

I shake my head. "This is not going to end well for them."

But when the door cracks open, it isn't answered by the Boneless King. Instead an ashen-faced ghoul with a plastic cup in his hand peeks out.

"We're here for the party," the French maid says uncertainly.

The ghoul looks them over. "Password?"

The maid quickly glances over her shoulder before leaning in. "Hades," she replies.

The ghoul waves his hand in a circle. "Come around through the alley. And keep your voices down till you're inside." He flicks his black-lined eyes at the buildings next door. "Nosy neighbors."

The maid and the buccaneer follow the instructions, and the door closes.

"At least we know the password," Viola whispers.

"Yeah," I say. But, of course, I'm not going to need it.

The alley is lined with puddles and large plastic trash bins. The maze of iron fire escapes overhead stifles the lamps in neighboring windows. We navigate it until we find the only light at all—a bare red bulb over the rear entrance to the Spite House. A vampire and King Neptune sit on the steps chatting, Neptune's trident resting across his knees.

I turn and stare Viola hard in the eyes.

"Viola, you need to stay *here*."

"Come on, Goyle," she protests. "You still don't think I can handle this?"

"This isn't some withering old Netherkin," I say sternly. "The Boneless King has powers over the dead, but he's also a threat to the living. His little visits to Hetty prove it. You need to stay here—for your own good."

"You don't know what you're walking into either," Viola points out.

"I'll take my chances."

"What if you need help?"

How can I make her understand? This isn't about me. This isn't about not wanting her by my side.

"Viola, I need you to promise. Promise me you'll stay put."

But Viola is suddenly distant, her eyes fixed on the door. She's hardly listening to me at all. Why must she be so difficult? Can't she see that, despite her stubbornness, and sarcastic words and white lies, for some strange reason I actually . . . care about her?

"Viola," I say again, and, reluctantly, I remove my hood from my head.

It catches her attention. I've never done this before. She's studying my wisp face, truly seeing it for the very first time. All my scars are visible now. Not just the chipped tooth and damaged brow, but the deeper ones. The ones I can't hide even as a wisp. My face is lined with worry. My cheeks are hollow with guilt. It's the face of a boy who's old beyond his years.

"Please," I implore her. "You're my friend. I don't want to lose another one. Promise me you'll stay."

Something in Viola's own face changes. Her eyes waver as they look into my own. And finally—reluctantly—she nods.

"You promise?" I say.

She nods again.

"Say it this time. Swear on your life."

Viola hesitates. Then, "I swear on my life." Her voice is barely a whisper, but I'll take it.

"Thirty minutes," I say, and slip my hood back over my head. "If I'm not back in half an hour, you turn and run. Don't look back. And don't return to Old Croak's or my Domain ever again."

I turn from her and walk past the chatty partygoers on

the step, and for a moment the red bulb overhead bathes me in a crimson glow.

I step inside. And find myself in a house of monsters.

The first floor is filled with more fiends and beasts than one would have thought possible to fit into such tight quarters. Granted, the monsters here aren't all that imposing, and the biggest threat seems to be that one might step on my toe or spill a drink in my lap. In the dim light of old-fashioned lanterns, I see pretend witches, fake zombies, and a glazed-eyed man in a straitjacket who may or may not actually need it. The otherworldly creatures mix and mingle with policemen and nurses, soldiers and cheerleaders. I spot the French maid and the buccaneer pushing their way to a steel basin filled with ice.

I feel something—the charged energy of the undead— but the press of too many human bodies is disorienting. My keen hearing works against me, and the roar of so many voices yelling to be heard overwhelms my senses. I feel the rhythmic beat of drums coming from somewhere. Overhead, I think. Through the maze of costumed revelers, I see a flight of narrow wooden stairs with a hand-carved wooden placard at its base. A string of small red lights illuminates its message.

COVEN ↑

I make my way through the masses and climb the narrow staircase, stepping around a pink-winged angel leaning her head against the banister. The second floor is darker and even louder than the first. No lanterns light this space, but a pulsing strobe bounces off the walls, casting everyone in green and blue hues. The throbbing drums I heard are electronic and come from the corner. A man in a long leather coat busies himself between two enormous speakers, ensuring there's no break in the macabre soundtrack. The dreadlocks under his top hat bob as he works, the tiny skulls that ring his hatband nodding in unison.

The partygoers here aren't talking. Paired off, they writhe and gyrate to the deafening beat. Some of them shut their eyes and seem lost in a world all their own. Their costumes are bleaker. Faces are painted white and lined in shadows to give the illusion of skeletal glares. The women's Victorian dresses and men's leather dusters smell aged and authentic.

The undead charge is stronger now. Again, my overloaded senses are unable to pinpoint the source, but I know I'm getting closer. Where the stairs continue up I see another red-lit sign.

BLACKENED VOODOO ↑

The third floor is pitch-black, its contents invisible except for the thick mob of dancing skeletons. Their white bones prance and glow in the darkness.

Somewhere overhead, an unseen black light obscures the dancers' head-to-foot costumes, highlighting only pearly ribs, shimmering skulls, and the long bones of limbs like cadavers come to life. The throb of drums is just as loud here, but their tone is no longer electronic. All around the room, a ring of skeletons has formed a drum circle, pounding their palms on the goatskin djembes tucked between their knees. The drummers' eyes are hollow and their jaws slack, as if in a trance.

Of course, the dancers can't see me, but they waggle their glowing jawbones in my direction before bobbing past. If I didn't know better, I'd think they were beckoning me to join them.

I feel the Boneless King. He's not here, but he can't be far. There's only one more floor.

The glowing white letters of a sign call to me from the base of the final flight of stairs.

HADES ♠

The attic is the smallest room of all. The heat of a hundred bodies below us has risen, giving it the feel of a furnace. Around me, the shadows burn crimson—a bare red bulb dangles down on a single cord strung from the rafters overhead. The drums are faint here; they might as well be miles away. A few wayward partygoers are curled up in the corner. They look to be asleep.

But my senses are a storm. The crush of energy almost buckles me.

I've finally reached the lair of the Boneless King.

He lounges just steps away on a throne of skulls and bone.

21

HADES

I see him now as I did that first night in the Fens. His featureless face is cocked toward a wiry shoulder as if perplexed to see me, but his hollow black eye sockets show no hint of surprise. The jagged, red-scrawled smile has smudged and his crown sits askew—giving him the look of a malevolent clown. The ends of his crimson scarf rest in his lap, his endless spindle legs sprawled in front of him and crossed at the ankles. All he needs is a heavy goblet in his fist to complete the image—a king lording it over this unseemly spectacle. But the sleeves of his ragged sweater just billow over the armrests of his undead throne and dangle toward the floorboards.

And yet, this time, his power is unmistakable. It radiates all around me in the tight space, as suffocating as hot brimstone. My head swirls. I'm flooded with fleeting images.

Dark earth and soil. Fingers crawling through the dirt. Unspeakable visions of the things this fiend has done over the years. To Samuel and other Bone Masons. To other Grotesques and the Twins. I can hear the pleas of those he's harmed. The creak of the bones on which he sits. And, finally, whether real or imagined, my mind's eye envisions what he intends to do to Hetty, and even little Tomás.

And then all I feel is rage.

The Boneless King's unflinching lipstick smile mocks me. I can't wait to wipe it off his vacant face.

I extend an open palm.

"The music's playing, Hannibal."

The Boneless King shifts his whole body at the sound of his given name, his head straightening, then tilting toward his other shoulder with curiosity.

"Aren't you going to dance?" I beckon with a finger, then clench my hand into a fist.

The Boneless King grips the arms of his throne and pushes himself up, the tips of his crown reaching all the way to the top of the arched rafters. He sways on his impossibly thin legs. His arms extend out to either side, the long sleeves of his moth-eaten sweater slip down past his wrist, and instead of hands, claws wriggle in the air.

I guess he's accepted my invitation.

I prepare to transform into my other wisp form—the one with the teeth and wings. The one best suited to punish. But I pause at the unexpected sight. The Boneless King's throne is now pulling itself apart, uncoiling as if coming to life. The intertwined skeletons untangle, rising up on their bony legs.

Netherkin.

I count six before the first one hurls itself at me with surprising speed. I catch it with a swat of my arm, sending it bouncing off the wall in a cascade of clattering bones.

But the rest follow quickly, teeth clacking as they snap and dig their hard fingers into me. Two more fall before I feel my arms pinned at my side. They won't be able to hold me for long, but they may not have to. The Boneless King is stepping forward, his arms long enough to stretch across the entire attic. His fingers probe like the legs of a black widow spider.

Another Netherkin falls as I free one arm, but I'd rather not face the Boneless King with one hand tied behind my back. As I slip free, the sharp tip of one of his fingers barely grazes my forearm, but the sting is beyond anything I've felt before. I leap away like a child who's scalded his hand on a hot stove.

I look down at the sleeve of my wisp form. It's sliced open. I don't bleed like you do, but I feel something unexpected—something leaking out from the fresh tear. I flex my hand and feel a weakening of my grip.

The Boneless King's painted mouth doesn't move, but his crooked smile sure looks smug.

I compose myself and ready for his next attack. I'm not one to sit back and wait, so I step forward to take the fight to him. But now my legs are stuck. One of the sleeping partygoers has wrapped his arms around my ankles. And now—ouch! He's sinking his teeth into my leg.

It's not a costumed practice-adult but another Netherkin. In the corner opposite me, two more push themselves up from their slumber. The Boneless King flicks his fingers and comes at me once more. I can't defend myself here—I need to lure him from this attic lair. I stomp the Netherkin at my feet and slowly back down the stairs to the black-lit room below.

It's loud and disorienting again, the drums still pounding. I'm aware of the glowing dancers around me, but my eyes are on the steps. The Boneless King and his Netherkin are following.

Something thuds hard against my shoulders. There's a painful clawing at my back. I turn and the skeletal dancers are swarming, hitting me from all sides. What is this? I can't touch or be touched by the *living*. When I reach out and block one's strike, I finally realize the truth—these aren't costumes at all.

I'm surrounded on all sides by even more Netherkin.

The Boneless King reaches the landing and lumbers forward, ducking to clear the ceiling.

I'm being slashed and torn at. There are too many—the space is too tight. This is a fight I can't win. I retreat, bullying my way through the dancing Netherkin as I hurry for the next flight of stairs. I shove aside a bony drummer and send his djembe flying.

Back on the second floor the partygoers are still packed shoulder to shoulder in their dreamlike states. At least they're not Netherkin. I've got a bit of breathing room, but not for long. My pursuers are close behind, pouring down the stairs and into the deafening noise of the crowded room. Dancers pulse green in the light of the strobe. They're lost in their music, but even if they weren't they couldn't see the chase unfolding before them. The strobe flicks and now the skeletal Netherkin glow red as they fan out around me, trying to pin me in.

The dreadlocked man in the skull-ringed hat suddenly

plucks his fingers and ratchets up the volume. The din sends my head spinning and the dancers shifting across the room. They unconsciously form a thick human wall, blocking the top of the last flight of stairs.

I curse them, but they can't be doing this on their own. Has the Boneless King gotten into their minds the same way he invaded Hetty's?

My exit blocked, I smash aside a Netherkin as I scan the room for another means of escape. Behind the dread-locked man, a thick black curtain shrouds a window. I have a clear path. I charge for it before the Netherkin can seal it off, just as the strobe light switches color again.

The room goes dark for a fraction of a second, and when the strobe flicks back on I check over my shoulder for pursuers. The dancers are cast in a hue of yellow-gold. I slam to a halt. There's a familiar face in the crowd. Her eyes are vacant and bewildered in the press of bodies, an out-of-place violin case still in her hand.

"Viola!" I yell in alarm, although she clearly can't hear me over the roar of the speakers.

I grit my teeth and hurry back for her. I kick the legs out from under one Netherkin as he rushes at me. I catch his thigh bone in midair and use it to knock the head off the next Netherkin right behind him. The skull goes clattering under a speaker.

"Viola!" I yell again as I reach her. But it does no good. Her gaze is behind me, over my shoulder. I recognize the same lost expression I saw on her face that night in Copp's Hill.

I glance back, following her eyes. The Boneless King has arrived from the floor above. He casts his hollow stare over the room and its throb of bodies, living and dead. He raises his hands and the black widow fingers click together. His arms lengthen and stretch well past the sleeves of his worn sweater, snaking around the walls of the room as if he's about to pull everyone here into his dark embrace.

I ready myself, then press my insides against my form with all my might. I feel like I might burst, but I know now that my wisp form is visible to anyone who looks my way. I hope it's enough to finally pull Viola from her trance. I lean in until I'm an inch from Viola's face, and boom as loudly as my voice will carry.

"Viola! We . . . must . . . go . . . *now!*"

Her eyes blink wildly, as if she's been yanked from a deep sleep. Then a flash of recognition. She gives me a shocked nod.

The window's no longer an option—the fall would crush her. I check the mob of dancers in front of the last flight of stairs. Their faces are now strained—as if all the undead energy around them is making them sick. I can't touch the living. But I can pass *through* them. Not that it will be pleasant for any of us.

"That way!" I say, pointing for the stairs. Making sure Viola follows, I press through the wall of bodies, feeling all their warm, squishy organs and flesh as my wisp form passes like a biting breeze. Yes, it's as awful as it sounds. The dancers squirm in discomfort, shifting their positions just enough for Viola to squeeze past too.

Back on the first floor the crowd has thinned, and I eye the exit to the narrow alley before opting for the unused front door. I've had my fill of tight spaces tonight.

We burst out onto the middle of the street.

Viola's face is like ice, paler than I've ever seen her. She looks like she might crack into shards right on the cobblestones.

"*Why* were you in there?" I ask, although my tone is more dumbfounded than angry. "Do you have any idea what could have happened to you?"

"I—I don't . . . ," she stammers. "I couldn't help it—"

Her explanation is interrupted by the clamor overhead. Shutters break and crash down onto the sidewalk. Netherkin are pouring from the windows of the Spite House. Black shadows now, they scuttle down the clapboards like angry wasps from a battered nest.

"Drop that foolish violin and run, Viola," I say sternly. "As fast as you can. Don't look back."

Viola's still disoriented but listens to me—in part. She rushes down the winding street with the violin case bouncing in her hand.

Free from the Spite House's oppressive confines, my senses are coming back to me. The Boneless King's energy has faded now that I'm free from his lair, and I watch as Viola disappears safely around a bend. I turn and brace my feet.

I feel like myself again.

I catch the first Netherkin with both arms and smash him over my knee. I snag another by his wrist, twist him high in the air, and snap him down on the asphalt like a wet towel. I grab a heavy trash can from the curb and use it to pummel several more.

I'm still in my visible state, and to any nosy neighbors watching from behind curtained windows, I must look like a sugar-crazed child throwing punches and kicks at imaginary foes.

But there's nothing imaginary about them. Finally, after I've cut through most of their numbers, the remaining Netherkin come to their senses and slink back into the gutters and sewers.

I check the surrounding alleyways one last time. To my

relief, Viola must have kept running. She's nowhere to be found. At the end of the street, a blue-and-white police car eases down the block. One of the neighbors must have made a call.

I narrow my eyes at the Spite House one last time, strobe lights glowing in its naked windows. It seems the Boneless King is still willing to bide his time inside. Whatever his reasons, I was lucky to make it out of that house of nightmares. Tomorrow is sure to bring with it many more.

Exhausted, I begin the long, damp walk in the drizzle back to my Domain.

Tonight's party may be over, but my job's far from done.

22

SHADOW MEN

My trudge home is bleak, the city as dark and brooding as my mood. As the fog of battle fades, the pain in my arm deepens. I finally have a chance to pause and examine my injury. The gash aches and oozes, a lingering reminder of the Boneless King.

I'm looking forward to returning to the comfort of my Domain, but when I arrive, dim lamplights peek out from ivy-covered windows.

Restless wards always ring alarm bells.

Instead of going straight to the roof, I make my rounds.

The Pandeys are awake, bickering with each other. A television drones in the Hairy Man's apartment. Miss Ada is cooking something. The cats are stirring behind the Korean lady's closed door.

My pace quickens. There's only one destination on my mind.

I reach the fourth floor, and my suspicion is confirmed. Hetty's apartment door is cracked open once again.

I know the Boneless King can't be here—now that I've felt his energy up close, I would have sensed him along the way. And if Netherkin have returned to pay a visit, they'll be disappointed to find an empty apartment. But that doesn't stop me from wanting to catch them in the act. I burst inside and look wildly from side to side.

The apartment lights are on. Someone is lying motionless on the couch. Her eyes are shut, mouth agape. Tiny speakers are stuffed in her ears and two dangling wires tether her to the glowing device in her lap. It's the blond practice-adult who tried to abduct me in the courtyard.

What's going on here? Nobody is supposed to be home. Where's Mamita? I look around hastily for an explanation. On the refrigerator, a list of emergency phone numbers is pinned under a magnet. I find a handwritten note on the kitchen table.

Good night, Hetty.

*Aunt Anna had to cancel. She had
a little accident but don't worry—
it's nothing serious. So sorry I can't
be there to tuck you in. Be good for
Courtney and take care of your brother.
I'll see you in the morning.*

Love you,
Mamita

That explains the presence of the practice-adult, and it means Hetty and Tomás should be in their beds. But there's something else here too. I feel nails on a chalkboard. By now, I bet even you can guess what it is.

I quickly check the body on the couch to see what they've done to her.

Is she . . . ?

I see the rise and fall of her sweater, the steady rhythm of sleep. That's a relief. But Mamita's questionable choice of babysitter is a problem for another day. I storm down the hall to Hetty's darkened bedroom. I hear the clink of tiny glass shards.

But when I fling the door open, even my guess is wrong.

Hetty is tossing and turning under her blankets, her face flushed but her eyes pinched tight. The sea glass wind chime sways in the window as if weathering a storm, but the air in the room is sour and still. And hovering over Hetty's bed is no normal Netherkin. It's a Shadow Man.

My old friend, the One in the Hat.

"You!" I say, my voice so bitter it comes out in a rasp.

The One in the Hat turns quickly, and I see the white slits of his eyes widen.

"Let me guess," I snarl. "I wasn't supposed to be here."

I suddenly suspect that feeble old Onesimus may be even more shrewd than I gave him credit for. Perhaps he had been serving the Boneless King in his own manner—directing me right into the jaws of a trap. Of course, it didn't matter whether or not I escaped the Spite House. The real plan was to lure me away from my Domain. *Aunt Anna had an accident.* Could the Boneless King's reach be long enough to have had a hand in that too?

I feel a creeping energy behind me. I turn quickly, and there's the Shadow Man's companion in the doorframe. The One with the Horns.

No matter. Neither of them will escape my Domain again.

I leap at the One in the Hat first—he's the closest threat to Hetty. I feel my grip tighten on his inky arm but he slips away in a cloud of vapor. I open my empty hand—it was the one weakened by the Boneless King's claw.

When the Shadow Man rematerializes behind me, he's assumed an entirely different form. Shapeshifters are pesky like that. But I'm in for another surprise. Standing before me is a man-sized, oil-slicked rabbit. His broken whiskers twitch and red eyes drill into me.

"Abracadabra," he says in a high-pitched churn of static, then offers a maniacal chuckle.

The Black Rabbit.

I remember Viola's story about Hannibal Craven and his assistant. The shadowy hat this persistent phantom has been wearing all these years? I recognize it now as a magician's top hat. It seems the Boneless King has sent his second-in-command.

"Pulling a rabbit out of a hat?" I say. "You really are a hack. The Magician? They should have called you the Clown."

He bares his oversized teeth but doesn't move.

"You're going to stay, are you?" I ask. "Good. But you'd better have a more impressive trick up your sleeve."

"No choice in the matter, little watchman," he cackles. "We can't leave empty-handed." His nose twitches and his unbroken ear cocks as if listening. "The Boneless King promises thrashings if we fail him again."

I've got some thrashings of my own in store for them.

I swipe at him, but he's as quick as, well, a rabbit.

He bounds out the door on his freakishly long legs and paws.

I try the One with the Horns, but he avoids me too and darts after the Black Rabbit. I must be losing a step. The night has taken its toll.

I check on Hetty. Her sleep is fitful, but she looks unharmed. I made it here without a second to spare. But now for the Shadow Men. I move to the hallway, hoping to intercept them before they can escape. But finding the hallway empty, I realize escape isn't the first thing on their mind.

We can't leave empty-handed.

Tomás!

I rush for his room just as I hear him burst into terrified tears. Amid a room filled with wicker baskets, stuffed animals, and cheerful pillows in hues of blue and green, the oil-streaked rabbit now looms monstrously over the crib, clutching something precious in his arms. His red eyes flare gleefully in the shadows cast by a tiny nightlight.

I'm hit hard. So hard the impact knocks me into the seat of a white rocking chair. The One with the Horns has attacked me from behind. My arm rages in pain. Strange. Strong Netherkin can cause me discomfort. In large numbers they can definitely slow me down. But seldom do they cause any real injury. I look down at the slice in my forearm made by the Boneless King. It's still seeping, and with a furious rush, the One with the Horns leaps upon me, thrusting a shadowy hand right through the wound.

I tumble backward in the chair, knocking down a shelf of diapers in a cloud of baby powder. The pain is excruciating. His fingers are digging inside me.

"Finish him off," the Black Rabbit orders the One with the Horns. "Do not fail the Boneless King." He tucks the glowing sphere of warm blue light under his arm and thrusts open the window sash.

Tomás isn't crying anymore. His little body lies still under his blanket, but he's not all there. The most important part of him has been stolen away.

But it's not too late. The Black Rabbit ducks through the window and extends one long leg onto the fire escape.

I lurch for him but freeze. The One with the Horns grips something inside my wisp body and squeezes, and I'm paralyzed with pain. Then he too shifts his shape, and I find myself smothered by the form of an enormous horned viper.

I shudder. A *snake*—it *had* to be a snake?

I try to drag myself toward the window, but he wraps

his black scaly coils around me and holds tight. The Black Rabbit clears the window, and I see his patchy haunches disappear.

I'm crushed. The pain is unbearable. But it's not the viper's squeeze that devastates me.

Not another ward. Not again.

"Tomás," I call helplessly at the empty window frame.

Then I'm blinded by a flash of raging light that engulfs the entire room.

23

THE SHADOW CATCHER

The One with the Horns slumps motionless on top of me.

I feel his grip falter, and he's torn away as if by some irresistible force. I blink to clear my eyes. He's no longer a viper, nor a Shadow Man. He's just a thick cloud of black tendrils swirling against a piercing white backdrop. A rudderless puff of acrid smoke caught in the wind.

Before my eyes, the cloud explodes into dust.

The room goes dark once again and I'm able to see.

Hetty stands in the doorway in her slippers and out-grown pajamas, her frame a small silhouette in the glow of the nightlight. She holds her sea glass wind chime in front of her like a lantern. The glass shards shiver and clink in her hand, then stop as if frozen. Completely still.

I've no time to ponder what just happened. I spring into action, hurling myself through the open window and onto the fire escape. The Black Rabbit is two landings below. One more and he'll make it to the street.

I throw my legs over the iron rails and let myself drop. My aim is true and I land on his shoulders. We both crash onto the landing.

I make it to my feet first. He staggers up, both ears now broken and dangling over his face from the impact. Before he can react, I swipe at the pulsing blue sphere, knocking it from his arms. Sorry, Tomás. That's sure to leave a scar somewhere down the road, but trust me—it's better than the alternative.

The Black Rabbit bares his teeth and moves for the sphere, and I decide it's best to put some more distance between them. I rush forward and bury my shoulders in his furry chest, sending us both tumbling off the fire escape and hard against ivy and brick. We skid down the wall in a rain of green leaves, landing on the pavement below.

I hit hardest, and this time the Black Rabbit is the first to his feet. He hovers over me and quickly lifts his huge black-nailed paw as if to stomp me. But he's not quick enough.

My face melts. My jaw unhinges. And just as the Black Rabbit brings his foot down, I swallow him up to his hip. Hopefully you've never heard the cries of a little cottontail caught in the teeth of a coyote. But just this once, it's music to my ears.

I fold him in half and devour the rest without chewing.

I carefully climb through Tomás's window and find Hetty leaning over his crib, trying to calm him.

"It's okay, Tomás," she whispers desperately. "It was just a dream."

But when she reaches down to stroke his forehead, he thrashes at her violently.

I look down at my uninjured arm, where I've safely cradled the delicate blue sphere. It pulses softly, like the gentle breath of a kitten. Strange how holding it makes *me* feel warm and comforted.

I creep quietly to the edge of the crib and place it in my hands. I cup open my palms, as if returning a tiny fledgling to its nest. The blue sphere glows bright and winks away, and Tomás is whole once again.

He still whimpers but has stopped his thrashing. He lets Hetty touch his foot, and it seems to bring him some relief. I head out of the room so I won't disturb them, glancing back just once as Hetty reaches into the crib and takes him in her arms.

"Come on," she whispers. "You can sleep with me."

She tiptoes to her room, sets him in the blankets, and curls up next to him. But both pairs of eyes remain wide and alert.

"It's okay," she whispers. "We've got each other."

No, Hetty. You've got more than that. And you're not spending the rest of the night alone.

I poke my nose around the corner of the doorframe.

Hetty sits up. "Clover?" she whisper-shouts.

I blink my big round eyes and wag my nubby tail. Then I trot in, jump on the bed, and curl up in a ball at their feet.

I don't sleep during the few remaining hours until daybreak. Hetty keeps her arms wrapped tightly around Tomás. If she dreams at all, the Boneless King has kept his distance—at least for one more night.

I hear Mamita arrive just before dawn, stirring Courtney awake and asking a few questions before sending her on her way.

Did they go down without a fuss? How did they sleep? Any problems?

Yes. Great. No, none at all.

I just shake my whiskers—adults and their narrow vision.

I hide under the bed when Mamita comes to check on the children. I see the look of concern in her dark eyes as she carefully eases Tomás from Hetty's embrace. She tucks Hetty's blanket under her chin and takes the baby to her own room for another hour of much-needed rest.

This exhausted family is teetering on the edge of collapse. I see it in Mamita's gait when she returns to wake Hetty for school. I feel it as Hetty sleepwalks through her morning routine. They're in an invisible war that they can't possibly understand. We won last night's battle—thanks in no small part to Hetty. How she did it, I still have no idea. But more Netherkin will be coming, and I don't think there are enough wind chimes in the entire city to stop them. I hope my presence here will be enough.

When Hetty's done dressing and brushing her hair, she eases her door shut and approaches me. She's looking at my forepaw.

"Clover, are you hurt?" she asks in concern. "Did you get in a fight?"

I hunker down and slink away before she can touch my leg. The fur is matted and slick from a weeping red gash, mirroring the one left in my sleeve by the Boneless King.

It's nothing, I want to say. *Just a little tussle.*

Hetty seems to sense that it's better not to push, and instead quickly retrieves her journal from the locked drawer. She plops herself down on her bed and begins sketching.

I watch her from my seat beside Mr. Jum-Jums. I notice the wind chime she's rehung in the window behind her, and for a moment, doubt it's the same one. The green and aqua glass shards have all turned brown, the color of mud.

"Do you like my Shadow Catcher?" she asks, looking up from the pages. "My father showed me how to make them. He said they catch bad dreams before they can scare you."

Yes, Hetty. In fact, I like it very much.

"I think it's about time to make a new one, though," she adds with a shrug, and returns to her journal.

"I don't know where you went, Clover," Hetty says without looking up from her writing. "But thank you for coming back."

From the kitchen, Mamita is calling. They're already late, and she needs to get Hetty off to school and herself to the hospital for the second half of her double shift.

Hetty climbs from the bed and moves to return her journal to the drawer. But she pauses, sets the journal on the desk, and places her palms on either side of the fishbowl.

Fin floats motionless on the surface of the water. His black fins have turned gray.

Coal miners used to bring caged canaries into the mineshafts. The delicate birds are particularly sensitive to invisible hazards, and a belly-up canary was a sure sign of danger in the air. Bad energy has a similar effect on small creatures. Have you ever had a pet fish or hamster keel over unexpectedly? I'd bet . . . well, never mind. They were probably just old.

Let's just say I'm surprised poor Fin made it this long.

Hetty's face falls and she bites her lip. "Who else is going to leave me?" she whispers.

From the other room, Mamita is imploring Hetty to hurry. The sadness in Hetty's eyes passes and she steadies her jaw. She picks up a little blue net, scoops the goldfish from the bowl, and marches toward the bathroom. She's strong, this one. Stronger than she should have to be at her age.

"Don't worry," I say as she eases the door shut. "I'm here until the end." But of course, she can't hear me.

I glance at the journal. Distracted, Hetty's left it open

on her desk. I hop on the chair and press my face to its pages to see this morning's pencil sketch.

It's a dog, with wide bulging eyes, perky ears, and a squashed nose. It's mostly black, with white along its belly and a little scar over one eye. I'm flattered to have made it into her journal, although I'd like to think I look a bit more ferocious in person.

Another sketch fills the opposite page. This one is more curious.

It's of a boy.

He wears a black ski vest and a coal-colored sweatshirt over slouched shoulders, hands thrust in his pockets. His face and head are obscured under a hood as if he's trying to disappear, but two intense eyes peer out from under the shadows of its folds.

Watching.

24

THE REMNANT

I return to my roof once Hetty and her family have left the apartment. They aren't the only ones who haven't slept, and I'd really like to crawl into my shell for some much-needed rest. But that's not why I'm here. Someone else is also on my mind.

Unfortunately, Viola doesn't come to see me.

Maybe I shouldn't be surprised. After all, I'm the one who told her to run and not look back. She's not my ward, and yet I worry for her almost as much as I do for Hetty and the residents of my Domain. I sit for a while under the overcast sky. Even more rain is on the way, I can smell it brewing out at sea. I watch the distant flight of the mother falcon as she stalks our glass-and-steel canyons, hunting pigeons for her chicks.

I hear a patter on the roof and perk up in anticipation. But it's not Viola. Just the first drops of rain. The patter becomes a steady drumbeat, then a pounding cascade as the skies open.

I try to formulate my plan. For tonight. And the next. Who knows what else the Boneless King has planned? The Netherkin will keep coming, and I've no choice but to match their pace. I should rest, regain my strength for tonight's troubles. But I can't. I need to see Viola—make sure she's safe. Once I do that, maybe I can focus on my real job. The threat to my Domain.

I venture into the storm as a wisp, navigating the puddles. The wind attacks umbrellas, turning them inside out. The water spills off the buildings in torrents, clapping at the pavement and rattling street signs. The roads are mostly deserted, a lost day for one and all.

Except for the gargoyles, that is. I pass a large fountain. Oh, how they preen, joyfully gargling the rain and whistling it through their silly puckered lips. Enjoy your moment of glory, you twits. Don't mind me, it's not like I could use any help fending off, what was it? Oh, yeah, an army of undead.

I reach Old Croak's and slip through the gap in the plywood sheeting. I feel a jitter of nerves in my stomach as I call for Viola—or maybe it's just the Black Rabbit slowly digesting in my gut. No reply comes as I step through the mounds of ash.

Descending the narrow back stairway, I feel my jitters increase. I expect to find her in the underground theater. On a day like this, she's unlikely to be outside. I creep into the Grotesque graveyard.

The theater smells mustier today, and I can hear drips of water from unseen cracks in the stucco ceiling. The broken bodies on the floor may never have become true Grotesques, but I show respect by carefully stepping over each one.

"Viola," I call. "Viola? It's me . . . Goyle."

Oh, bricks, she's even got me using that name now.

But there's still no reply. I check behind the crumbling pillars and make my way up to the balcony. I don't find her curled up sleeping in some abandoned seat. Perplexed, I sigh and rest my elbows on the railing as I stare down at the theater. Where else could she have gone? Perhaps, for once, she actually followed my instructions. Maybe she'll never return here or to my Domain again.

But below, on the stage, hidden behind some unused boxes, I spot the familiar object resting like a little black coffin. I rush back down to the main level and hurdle onto the stage, skipping the steps. I blink to make sure I'm not mistaken.

Viola's violin case. Alone. Abandoned.

I anxiously cast my eyes over the shadows. Maybe she's hiding, afraid that I'm upset at her for following me into the Spite House last night.

"Viola! If you're here, come on out. I'm not mad. *Really*. I just want to see you. I've come to make sure you're all right."

I'm answered by silence.

"Viola!" I bellow this time, my concern rising. Of course, my voice doesn't echo. If anyone else were present, it might sound like the faint rustle of old sheet music.

Never once have I seen Viola without her case. What possibly could have possessed her to leave it behind now? Suddenly I'm afraid. Did one of the Netherkin slip past me outside the Spite House? Could they have followed her here?

I crouch down, the case's brass fasteners just inches from my touch. I've come to accept that there's no violin in there. I'm quite certain that this is where Viola keeps her belongings. A blanket, maybe. Some spare change. A toothbrush, I hope. But also maybe a clue as to where she might have gone?

I undo the clasps and the case falls open. Nothing but a worn felt lining greets me. The case is entirely empty.

Except, that is, for a single, silky string.

Not fishing line. Certainly not dental floss. It shines clear and strong.

Probably, it's nothing. And yet I'm overwhelmed by the urge to touch it. I carefully extend a finger and press it against the fiber.

The jolt is like lightning, and I'm overwhelmed by a surge of memories stronger and more vivid than I've ever experienced before.

I'm in a bed, warm and comforting. It's not my Domain— I don't hear the sounds of the city. I smell animals. Livestock. Grain and lavender. The room is dark, the shutters drawn, but a sliver of bright sunlight peeks under the sill. There's a pail of water beside the bed. A moist sponge on the mahogany nightstand.

Around me there is music. Gorgeous, beautiful music. Just one instrument. A violin. I look up and see a man seated on a stool by the bed. His face is lined and tired, skin bronzed from the sun and his hair flecked gray. He doesn't wear the tuxedo or tails of a concert performer.

There's soil under his nails, his thick hands callused from labor. His eyes are shut as he plays.

My body is small and weak. I'm aware of pain from head to foot, but at the moment any discomfort is dull and far away. This memory is no nightmare. All I feel is relief, basking in this precious little moment of happiness.

The notes soar, carrying me with them on their ebb and flow. When the violinist finishes the song, he opens his eyes and sees me watching. He smiles.

In this tired man's face I feel an emotion. One that's powerful, steadfast, and raw. It's foreign to me, and yet I somehow know what it is.

In that moment, I know that I am loved.

A roar jars me from my vision. I'm in the underground theater again, a subway car rumbling through some nearby tunnel.

Disoriented, I lift my finger from the string. It's like I've been yanked away forever from some wonderful journey. I don't know how long I was gone—it could have been minutes or hours. It takes me a moment to regain my senses, and as much as I would like to return and linger there, I know I need to get back to my Domain. These days, night comes all too quickly.

Reluctantly, I close the violin case and fasten the clasps. I want to take it with me but feel I should leave it for Viola in case she returns. Only she can explain what it is—and what it means. If I don't find her by tomorrow, I'll come get it myself.

I return to my Domain under wet, gloomy skies. When I arrive at the entrance I look up and see a glow in Hetty's bedroom window. She's home from school and it's the type of dark afternoon that calls for lamplight. I head upstairs to check on her but stop before shifting into Clover. The apartment door is cracked open again. I feel a familiar hum in the air. Not as intense as recent nights, but ominous nonetheless.

Not *again!* What sort of Netherkin dares to walk by day?

I tear through the apartment and burst into Hetty's room. She's in her bed, lying peacefully on her side, closed eyelids fluttering gently.

And sitting next to her on the edge of the bed is ... someone.

Her hands are folded neatly in her lap over striped leggings. She's leaning close to Hetty's ear, whispering—her lips so pale they're almost transparent. The words are more of a ripple in the air than an actual voice. I recognize the newsboy cap and the crimson-streaked pigtail tucked behind an ear.

But now I recognize even more—the most obvious feature, which I've somehow overlooked.

An uncontrollable fury rises up inside me. I step forward before she realizes I'm there. I reach out and clutch Viola by the neck. Her body stiffens in my grip.

And now I know for certain. I'm such a stupid block of stone.

I can't touch or be touched by the living, but she's not alive.

Viola is a Netherkin.

25

VIOLA

I press Viola against the wall by her throat. I'm so angry I'm speechless, not that I don't give it a try.

"You!" I bark. "You *lied* to me!"

"Goyle, please," she gasps. "Let me explain." Her fingerless gloves desperately grab at my hands.

"Has this been your plan all along? Fool me so you can get to Hetty?"

"Yes," she says, and coughs as my grip tightens. "I mean, yes *and* no. Not for the reasons you're thinking."

"I've had more than my fill of Netherkin this week,

Viola. They're practically bursting out my ears. But I've got room for one more."

"Then do it, Goyle!" she shouts, her eyes flashing. "I've done what I needed to, so go ahead and swallow me if that will make you happy!"

"It doesn't make me happy at all," I protest. "I thought you were my friend."

"I *am* your friend," she chokes. "I came here to help Hetty. And if you can get past your blind hatred and listen to me for five minutes, I think I can help you too."

I loosen my fingers but don't let go. "Another tall tale from the violin-playing Netherkin?"

Viola's eyes flare. "It's not a tall tale. If I wanted to hurt Hetty I would have done it when I got here an hour ago."

I open my hand and Viola falls to the floor.

How could I have been so blind? No wonder she can see and speak with me. And now that I think about it, I've never actually seen her talk to a living person at all. All the clues have been staring me right in the face. Viola's mysterious appearance on my roof. Her miraculous escape in the subway. The hands on my back under the Copper Dragon? They were hers, I was just too lost in rage to realize it.

"You and Onesimus are exactly the same," I fume. "All you Netherkin are—what do they call it these days?— phony bolognas."

"No, we're not all the same." She pushes herself up from the floor. "And *nobody* uses that expression, by the way."

I sputter my lips at her. It comes out as a growl.

"It's true, Goyle. I don't blame you for thinking otherwise—you were *made* to believe that way."

"What do you mean by that?" I ask. "I'm warning you, Viola. Your next insult will be your last."

"The Bone Masons made you despise all Netherkin because they didn't know if they could trust you. It's the same reason you can't touch the living or enter your wards' dwellings without being invited."

"Why wouldn't they trust us? We're dedicated, loyal, brave—" I could go on and on, but Viola interrupts me.

"Yes, yes, I know all that, Mr. Humble. But once your stone form is set, you're on your own. The Masons can't communicate with you. They don't know what you're thinking. Every Grotesque is going to outlive his Maker many times over. What happens if your mind-set changes over time? How are they supposed to know that you won't harm those you were built to protect?"

"I'd never do that," I scoff. "I can't even imagine it."

"Exactly," Viola says. "Because they infused you with these absolute beliefs and values. But the Bone Masons aren't all-knowing. Times change. Some rules that make sense most of the time, or made sense long ago, don't *always* apply."

My mind is reeling. Was I so lonely, so desperate for a friend—any friend—that I only saw what I wanted to?

"Why didn't I sense you before?" I waggle my fingers at her. "Where's all your static and nasty Netherkin vibrations? Are you covering it up with some sort of black magic?"

"*I'm* not here to harm your wards. That's what I'm trying to tell you. You didn't sense me because I'm *not* a threat."

I glare at her. In the short time I've known her, Viola's shown herself to be as guarded as a keystone and as unbending as a pillar. But in truth, she's never been dangerous to anyone but herself.

"Think about it," she implores. "If I came here to hurt your wards, why would I help Tomás outside the playground? Why would I push you to get inside this apartment and find out what was going on with Hetty?"

Admittedly, I can't come up with any easy answers to those questions.

"Don't you get it yet?" she asks, throwing her hands in the air. "You don't sense Netherkin because they're *dead*. You sense them if they're *bad*. And not all Netherkin are bad, Goyle."

I open my mouth to protest, but hesitate. I never really thought about it that way before. I always just assumed . . . I mean, it made perfect sense that . . .

I shake my head at the muddied thoughts.

"Then why deceive me?" I say. "How was that helpful?"

"I lied so you would give me a chance. If I'd told you what I was that very first night, would you ever have let me off your roof?"

Probably not, although I don't admit it. "You could have told me later," I grumble.

"I *tried* to tell you yesterday!" she says. "I tried to tell you everything at Old Croak's and again outside your friends' chapel, but you cut me off. You were so busy cursing Netherkin I didn't know what you might do."

My boil has eased to a simmer, but I'm not ready to let her off the hook just yet.

"Did you even really help out around the shop?" I scoff. "Or is that just part of your made-up story? Maybe *you* were one of the Netherkin who started that fire."

It's a halfhearted accusation that I don't really believe myself, but Viola's porcelain face goes hard. She's quiet for a long while. Her gaze drops to Hetty's colorful throw rug, then moves back to me. When her eyes meet mine, I see they've gone wet.

"I died in that fire, Goyle," she says. "Right alongside Hetty's father."

I stop. Her words hit me like a hammer and chisel. For the first time, it occurs to me that Viola has lost something precious too.

This time, my words are the ones that come slowly.

"*Can* you move on to what's Next?"

She nods.

"Then why are you still here?" I ask. "Why choose to stay?"

"Because Samuel was there to help me when nobody else would. Now it's my turn to return that kindness. Who else can help Hetty, other than me ... and you?" Viola glances at Hetty, then back again. "I'm no Grotesque, Goyle. But maybe *I'm* just trying to give new purpose to a life cut far too short."

We're interrupted by a wavering, dreamy voice.

"Excuse me?"

Viola and I both turn to the bed in surprise.

Hetty is sitting up in her blankets, studying me with a look of recognition. Her eyes are open, but far away and unfocused. *"You,"* she says. "You're the boy who helped me and Tomás last night."

I shake my head, dumbfounded. Holy bricks, is Hetty a Netherkin too?

"Of course not, silly," Hetty says, stunning me even further.

She can *hear* my thoughts?

"I can see and hear people like you in my dreams,"

she explains sleepily. "I've been able to ever since I was a little kid."

I look back at Viola in disbelief.

"Why are you trying to hurt that nice girl?" Hetty asks.

"I . . . I wasn't," I mumble. "I mean, it was just a misunderstanding."

"Oh, that's good," Hetty says. She yawns and folds her hands in her lap. "Do you think you guys could keep it down while you sort it out? I'm trying to take a little nap. I haven't been sleeping well, and tonight's Halloween, you know."

"Yes, that's right," I say. "I'd nearly forgotten. Sure, we'll try to be quieter."

"Thank you." Hetty lies back down, tucking her hands under her cheek and settling onto her pillow. "Oh, by the way," she says. "If you happen to see a little black-and-white dog around, could you send him this way? It's a big city out there and I'm worried about him."

I give her a nod. "Sure, I'll do that. Sorry for waking you."

"No problem." She settles in and closes her eyes. "I'll hardly remember any of this when I wake up, anyway."

26

ARMY OF ONE

The sun has barely set on this late afternoon. The lights in the glass tower on Boylston Street cut through the foggy sky. They've lit the windows in a pattern that forms a giant jack-o'-lantern in celebration of Halloween. Its jolly, snaggletoothed smile greets the city.

The sidewalks below are already lined with tiny monsters and demons. Fairies and princesses too. The youngest tricksters have taken to the streets, accompanied by their umbrella-toting parents. Viola and I watch them stumble in their oversized costumes, on their way to kiddie parties or to trick-or-treat in the safety of a neighbor's familiar building. We dangle our legs over the edge of the roof.

"Did you ever dress up for Halloween?" I ask. "I mean, before . . ."

"Of course, when I was small."

"As what?" I ask.

"Different things. My favorite was a witch."

I look at her crossed arms, striped leggings, and knee-high, no-nonsense boots. The cocked cap shadows her eyes.

"Didn't take too much effort, I bet," I offer. The frost between us has thawed—slightly.

She narrows an eye. "Yeah, well, it was a long time ago."

"It's strange seeing you without your violin case."

She just nods.

"I found it," I mention.

"I hoped you might," she says. "Did you look inside?"

This time, *I* just nod.

"What did you think?" she asks.

"It was . . ." I remember the brief but extraordinary journey. I can still feel the sensation. "I don't know how to describe it."

"You don't have to," Viola says.

"Was that my Remnant?"

She nods again.

"What were you doing with it?"

"Like I said, the Bone Masons pass them down from one generation to the next. I wanted to hang on to it for safekeeping. So I could show it to you when the time was right."

"I saw a man—when I touched it. He was playing the violin. I was sick, I think, and he was comforting me. Do you know what that could have meant?"

Viola offers a tight smile. "I have an idea, Goyle. But only you will know for certain. When this is all done, I'll do my best to help you understand."

Her answer piques my curiosity, but I'm nothing if not patient. A hundred and thirty years on a roof will do that to you.

"What were you whispering to Hetty?" I ask. "In her bedroom."

"Oh, just girl talk," she says coyly. I scowl in reply.

"Okay, I was telling her the truth. About the Bone Masons. And about what really happened to her father. Samuel always kept his family as far removed from his craft as possible. It's become far too dangerous an occupation, and he had no intention of seeing his children follow in his footsteps. For all they knew, he was a simple stone carver."

I cock my head. "Then why bring them into it now?"

"Because the Boneless King obviously doesn't care about intentions. *His* intention is to wipe out the entire family line, just to be safe." Viola pauses and casts her eyes out at the city. "Besides, Hetty is special. You saw it for yourself." She turns to me and holds my gaze. "Imagine a Bone Mason who can communicate with Grotesques. Who can see and understand *your* world, Goyle, the world you've been thrust into. Just imagine what a Maker like that could do."

"You want her to become a Bone Mason like her father? Wasn't he trying to protect her from all that?"

Viola sets her jaw. "I want her to be safe. That's what Samuel would have wanted. She can't stay safe if she keeps living in the dark. What she does with the information now—that's entirely up to her."

I wonder what I might do in Hetty's shoes.

"I'm sorry I lied to you," Viola says again. "But if you'd known I was a Netherkin you would never have let me near her."

I can't disagree with her. But it's funny—for just a moment, I'd entirely forgotten that I was sitting and talking to a Netherkin.

"Did you tell her anything else?" I ask.

"I did." Viola hesitates. "I told her a few things about you."

I raise a curious eyebrow.

"And I think I'll keep most of that to myself. Just so I don't embarrass you," she adds with a smirk. "But the gist of it is this. I told her not to worry. Because she's not alone."

I study the darkened skyline. The smiling jack-o'-lantern on the glass tower stares back at me.

"She may not be alone, Viola, but *I* am. I felt the power of the Boneless King in his lair. I barely escaped. He'll send his Netherkin tonight. And tomorrow and the next. He'll keep at it until I can't fight them off anymore. And even if I do, eventually he'll grow strong enough to come himself. For Hetty, and everyone else." I look down at the wound in my arm. "I don't think I can destroy him. The Twins couldn't do it. The Bone Masons and Grotesques that tried before me couldn't either."

"You're right, Goyle, you can't destroy him. Not without his Remnant."

I turn to her, hopeful. "You know where it is?"

"Of course not. I just swept floors and nosed around in journals."

So much for words of encouragement.

"But you don't need to destroy him," she continues. "You just need to hurt him. Put him back in the ground like they've always done before, and buy everyone some time."

I shake my head. "I tried to at the Spite House. He was strong. Too strong."

"That's why you need to get him *here*. Where you're at your strongest and while he's still weakened. That's your best chance."

"Bring him *here*? What if I fail?"

Viola shifts on the roof, tucking her legs underneath her and pivoting to face me.

"Goyle, do you know why Hetty and her family moved to this building? Because Samuel insisted that if anything ever happened to him, they needed to come here. Why do you suppose that is?"

I shrug. Viola leans in closer.

"Because of *you*. Samuel knew you guarded this Domain. He knew you could protect them. He believed in you."

"I'm just one Grotesque. The Boneless King has an army."

"Cut down the Boneless King and his army will scatter like frightened flies."

The risk seems enormous, but what choice do I have?

"How do you suggest I get him here?" I ask. "Time's on his side . . . not mine."

"I've been thinking about that," Viola says. "He's arrogant. And he thinks he already has you beat. Goad him.

Make him angry." She gives me a sly smile. "You're a snarky little bag of rocks when you want to be. Send him a message and get under his skin."

"I do have a way with words," I agree. "But who will deliver the message? For Hetty's sake, I can't leave my Domain again."

Viola stops and sets her jaw. "I'll do it. He's been trying to draw me to him anyway—like all the others. The night in the cemetery and again at the Spite House. I've felt it every time we've gotten close to him."

"He'll destroy you. Or make you one of them."

"How bad could it be?" Viola says with a nervous chuckle. "I'm already dead."

She could end up like Onesimus. Trapped in this world, rotting forever. Or worse. I've heard the fear in the voices of the other Netherkin when they speak of the Boneless King. I won't let that happen to her.

"No, that won't do," I say. I pinch my lips between my fingers. "But there is another option."

I gag and retch. I feel like one of the cats downstairs trying to cough up a hairball.

"Are you all right?" Viola asks. "You're sure about this?"

I'm standing with my hands on my knees, my mouth agape. I raise a finger to indicate one more try.

I cough and heave, my stomach contracts, and something soft and sick-tasting finally rides up my throat and past my lips. I deposit it in a slimy mass on the rooftop.

Viola grimaces and covers her mouth. "Oh, that's vile. Worse than hot apple filling."

I wipe my brow and straighten up. "How do you think *I* feel?"

The Black Rabbit squirms on the ground in front of us. But he doesn't look at all like a rabbit anymore. He's just a small quivering mass of undigested black fur and ooze. I can barely make out an ear, and the remains of a single red eye.

"I *think* there's something left of him there," I say. "Good thing my metabolism's not what it used to be."

Viola just shakes her head and looks away.

"Can you hear me?" I yell at the pile. "If so, wave. Or, I don't know, blink or something."

What's left of the Black Rabbit gurgles. His red eye trembles.

"Good. It's your lucky day, Magician. I'm sending you back to your Boneless King."

A thin puddle of slime seeps from the mess like a feeble tentacle.

"Uh-uh. Not so fast. I've got a message for you to

deliver." I crouch back down, my hands on my knees again, and look the Black Rabbit square in his solitary eye.

"You tell the Spineless Prince that I'm here waiting for him," I growl. "If he wants my Domain—and my wards—come and get them. But tell that wriggly oyster I plan to wash him down with a lemon and a shot of Tabasco."

The Black Rabbit bubbles and simmers.

I pause and think of something more. "And tell him I'm going to use his silly paper crown to wipe my—"

"Goyle!" Viola interrupts.

"What, too much?" I ask. I shrug and return my glare to the Black Rabbit. "That's all, then. Go on."

The Black Rabbit spreads out into a pool on the roof, meekly fumbles for the edge, and oozes down the side.

I wipe my mouth, cross my arms, and give a nod of satisfaction.

"Well, that should do it," I say.

"You're okay with letting him go?" Viola asks.

I shrug. "The ugly bunny's been a hairball in my throat all day," I say.

But despite my bluster, I have no idea where the night will lead us. I drop down on the parapet and try to settle my stomach.

Viola sits with me for a long while. We don't say much. It just feels good to have a friend by my side.

The night darkens. Rush-hour traffic ebbs. Finally, I tell her, "It's time for you to go."

"I don't have to, Goyle. I can stay here with you."

"No, Viola. You've done enough. Really, move on while you still can."

She doesn't get up.

"Please, Viola. Even you know you're helpless against the Boneless King. But you've helped me realize that maybe I'm not."

Viola reluctantly rises to her feet. This time, when she leaves, she heads for the stairs of my Domain. My chest tightens. She hasn't even left and already I miss her. There's something more I need to admit.

"Viola," I call after her, then hesitate. I swallow hard. "I don't know if I can do it."

When she pauses, the words I've been holding back for so long tumble to the surface. "I'm all by myself. I'm ..."

I exhale deeply and pull the last word like a splinter. "Afraid."

Viola lingers for a moment. When she walks back to me, her eyes hold my own.

"It only takes an army of one," she says softly. "If the one is strong enough."

Viola puts her hand on my mauled forearm. I flinch. Not in pain, but in surprise. Her touch of reassurance is a new sensation for me. Then again, maybe it's not. It's just been so long, I've forgotten how it feels.

"And you are," she whispers.

And with that, Viola disappears.

It's almost time. The dark energy is building, clouds ready to burst overhead.

I slip into the stairwell and punch the glass of a little red fire alarm on the wall. I pull its handle, and my Domain erupts into a chorus of sirens.

I feel bad sending my wards into the rain, but they'll be safer outside. This is no false alarm.

I sit alone on the edge of my roof for what might be the last time. The towering electric jack-o'-lantern grins back at me from across the cityscape. Rain pounds. Streetlights dim. The siren echoes up and down the hallways of my Domain.

The Boneless King is coming.

27

THE BONELESS KING

He arrives like a hurricane that's been building energy at sea, and brings with him a hundred-year storm. Dark clouds, heavy and bruised, descend and fill our asphalt valleys, muting the glow of buildings and traffic lights. Even the electric jack-o'-lantern wavers behind the fog.

The sky opens, soaking my poor wards huddled on the sidewalk. They take shelter under awnings and eaves as they wait for the fire trucks to arrive. I spot Hetty and see she's still in her Halloween costume. She wears a workman's apron, her hair tucked under a wool cap that looks a lot like Viola's. In her hands are a mallet and chisel. Under her nose, a curly black mustache drawn with eyeliner now runs down her face. I'd bet my tail she's dressed as her father. Tomás rides in his mother's arms wearing a yellow slicker and white skipper's cap—Captain Poopy-Pants. Hetty's idea, no doubt. I smile, but I have no time for light thoughts.

I walk to the middle of my roof just as the whole building begins to tremble. An electric charge is spreading from floor to floor. There's no need to peer over the edge. I know there's a nightmare crawling up the side.

I turn my back. I don't want the Boneless King to see my face. Not yet. Not until I can control the storm swirling inside me. My mind flashes to the Twins. I never saw what he actually did to them, but it grows more and more horrible as my imagination fills in the blanks. I remember all the Netherkin he's sent to my Domain, especially the vile Shadow Men. My temper rises as I think of their filthy hands on Tomás, and of what they might have done to Hetty. And I replay their visits before, to the ward I let slip away. I try to temper all these thoughts—they leave me reeling as if I might burst. But I can't tame them.

I'm just an angry boy, standing here in my hoodie and vest. But tonight, I'm all my wards have got. I clench my fists and turn to face the Boneless King.

A long arm slaps down over the side of the roof,

probing fingers scuttling like spider legs as they search for a grip. The sharp claws find what they seek, leaving deep gouges in my rooftop as the Boneless King pulls himself up and over the edge. When he stands on his wobbly legs, he towers even taller than when I faced him in the Spite House.

Behind him, on rooftops across the city, I see eager shadows. The vague forms of Netherkin peer from gables and gutters but keep their distance. It seems they've gathered for the show.

If I were some comic book hero I might exchange witty words with the Boneless King, tell him his time is up. But tonight I'm no hero, just a rash *terrible child*. I charge without warning and hurl myself against him. He staggers on stiltlike legs, but I'm the one who feels like I've rushed headlong into a deep-rooted tree.

The Boneless King catches me under my arms and throws me aside with ease. He's stronger than I ever imagined, but I quickly regain my feet.

The Boneless King cocks his head, regarding me curiously as he's done before. But his head snaps forward violently as I interrupt his thoughts. I've caught the end of his long crimson scarf, dangling on the rooftop. With a mighty tug I yank it like a rope and send him tumbling crown over heels across the roof until he smashes hard into

the door of the stairwell. His knees buckle and he collapses into a pile of rubbery limbs.

Now I know I can hurt him.

I drop the end of the scarf and rush for the cinder block
the practice-adults use to prop the door. I take it with both
hands and hoist it over my head.

But before I can bring it down, a vinelike arm whips
up, fingers slashing my face. I drop the block and press my
hand to a leaking gash on my cheek. As soon as I do it, I
realize I've made a mistake. I feel a sudden thud and hear
a pop. The pain is so excruciating my vision blurs.

I glance down. The spider fingers of the Boneless King
have punched straight through my vest and out the other
side. I look back up at his motionless red smile. He too
knows I've made a fatal error.

I drop to my knees.

The pain ebbs when his fingers slither back through
the fresh hole, but I feel my wisp form spilling all around
me. The Boneless King bends a knee and kicks me with
all his might. The impact sends me across the roof until
I come to rest on my chest, my cheek pressed against the
ground.

On distant rooftops, Netherkin titter and sway in anticipation.

I do not know what comes Next for a Grotesque. I

don't know what comes Next for you either. But I'm about to find out. If there's a way to fill you in, I promise to come back and tell.

I see the laceless boots of the victor clopping toward me now. He's readying his final blow. Boneless King, it seems I've underestimated you.

But he halts his march. His head wobbles back like a dog at the end of its leash, and he looks to the ground in agitation.

"Goyle!" I hear a voice shout.

I raise my head with the last of my strength. It can't be.

Viola! She must have dropped onto my rooftop from the neighboring building. I see she's pinned the trailing end of the Boneless King's long scarf under her boot. She's calling something. "Use your—"

The Boneless King turns at the sound of her voice. I want to call back to her. Tell her it's too late. Plead for her to run.

But the Boneless King is quicker than both our voices. One of his arms slashes like a twisted tentacle, and the black widow claws strike Viola. Her eyes go wide and her words die in her throat as the impact knocks her against the neighboring wall in an explosion of gray smoke.

I scream in anger and roll, tangling myself in the Boneless King's spindly legs. The impact buckles him and he falls to the ground. Somehow I mount him and batter his head weakly with my fists. But I feel his other arm wrap around my body, and he easily throws me to the edge of the roof.

I'm on my back. I can no longer feel my arms or legs. I look, and I see the gashes and holes in my wisp body, my energy leaking into deep puddles. Sirens wail. The sky around me flashes red. The fire trucks below light up the street.

Unbelievably, I hear a voice again. Frail. Broken. Barely a whisper, but still there.

"Goyle," Viola says, crawling on her hands and knees. I'm relieved to see her, but she's in as bad shape as I am. Her hat's gone, pigtails loose over her face. Her pea coat is charred black and still smoldering.

She's able to raise a finger and force two more words.

"Monster up."

I look where she's pointing.

My shell is right above me.

It's the means of last resort. If I take it, the clock starts running—I won't have much time. And I'll only get one chance. If I fail in my stone form I'll be rendered helpless, leaving Hetty and everyone else at the mercy of the Boneless King. But what option do I have left?

With the last bit of my wisp energy, I flash into my stone body.

The Boneless King has unwrapped his scarf and tossed it angrily on the ground. His head bobs on a scarred and sickly pencil of a neck as he searches for me. Then he turns to the parapet and sees for himself.

Already, I feel my armor strengthening me. The wounds of my wisp form fill as hard as rock. My mind surges with renewed energy and dark visions. What the Boneless King has done to the Twins. To Hetty and Tomás. And now to Viola. Everyone I hold dear. The anger pulses. But this time, I realize it doesn't help me. Anger can only hurt.

I compose myself. The images fade away. I ball up my rage and tuck it somewhere far away, until all I'm left with is calm. And the awareness of who I am.

I am Penhallow. The Night Warden of this Domain. This is my job, and I do it well.

But no, I'm more than that now. I am the guardian of this entire city.

Rain drips off my stone chin. I clench and stretch my jaws. Eyes open, shimmering like wet marble. My wings unfold after so many years and I rise from my crouch.

I feel awake. Alive. Like the falcon that stalks these glass-and-steel canyons.

The Boneless King rushes forward. I meet him head-on. This time, when we collide he's the one who buckles backward. I'm now denser and heavier than he is, but he still has the advantage of height and reach.

He keeps out of range of my powerful claws and jabs from a distance with his limber arms and razor fingers. I tense my powerful haunches and launch myself forward, barreling through his defenses. But his power is still growing and I'm lifted into the air. I see his paper crown and the rooftop swirling under me before he wrenches me downward with all his might.

The roof buckles and gives way. I crash right through in a rain of bricks and plaster, coming to rest in a heap on the floor of the vacant apartment below.

I stare up at the hole overhead. I don't budge as the rain patters down on me and the surrounding debris.

I can't move, I repeat silently to myself. *I'm stuck here.* As if my thoughts might be enough to convince him.

The Boneless King hovers over the gaping hole in a swirl of dust. He reaches carefully down into the apartment, long black fingers probing. His nails still bite, but they no longer sink in. He'll have to come closer for that. And to his surprise, I'm going to let him.

He leaps into the hole, landing hard on top of me. He bores his nails into my granite shoulders until they lodge there—tight. His painted mouth is still fixed in its wicked grin.

I allow myself to smile too.

Does this trick sound familiar?

This time, it's the Boneless King who has taken my bait.

"Sticks and stones may break *others'* bones," I sing, then flash a menacing, cracked-tooth smirk. "But *I'm* a Grotesque, Hannibal Craven."

I sink my own stone claws into his fleshy mass.

My heavy wings beat. They're out of practice but don't fail me. The Boneless King is a creature of the underground—of suffocating earth and fallow soil. My Domain is the rooftops—and the sky above them. We explode up out of the apartment, through the hole, and leave the roof below us.

The Boneless King struggles to free his fingers from my body, but I don't return the favor, and the talons on my feet clutch his waist even tighter.

My Domain disappears, the fire trucks and assembled crowd shrinking with every second. I soar high above the buildings, streets whirling far below. I feel the Boneless King's nails scraping and clawing my back in desperation.

I remember the falcon again as I look toward her roost atop the glass tower. The electric jack-o'-lantern seems to grin and offers his approval. I pin back my ears and dive. We smash right through his front teeth in a shower of glass.

Now we're inside, hurtling through a dark labyrinth of hallways and cubicles. I don't let us touch the carpet even as our bodies are battered by desks and chairs. File cabinets bounce off us with a rain of paper, but I won't let go—they do far more damage to the Boneless King than to me.

I'm a wrecking ball, exploding fluorescent bulbs and shattering an entire glass conference room. I crumble a wall. Out of the corner of my eye, I see two yellow imps pause from nibbling telephone wires. They look up in awe and disbelief.

Enjoy the show, fellas, you're not on the menu tonight.

The Boneless King struggles furiously, but I ignore the pain and beat my wings even harder.

We burst through the other side of the tower and find ourselves in open air once again. My strength is beginning to wane, but our ride's almost over. I rear back and we soar vertically, rocketing up past the building's highest floors until we clear the blinking lights of the radio antennas on the roof. Over the cityscape now, the dense clouds are lifting, and the city's tallest peaks fan out in a forest of lights. I see the harbor and the islands beyond it.

The Boneless King's voice rumbles deep within my core.

"Enough, monster! Put me down!"

I stop our ascent, and for a moment we just hover. I stare into his bottomless eye sockets.

"Funny," I say. "I was thinking the same thing myself."

I retract my claws and let him go.

He plummets in a spiral of arms and legs, his paper crown flying from his head and sailing away on the breeze.

His unflinching red smile hurtles past the glass tower and deep into the concrete canyon, until he hits the pavement with the sound of a thunderclap. The impact sends him through the sewers and subway tunnels—beyond the deepest foundations of the city. When the Boneless King finally comes to rest, there's no evidence left of him at all except for a mysterious crater as wide as a city bus.

And his little paper hat.

I watch the lost crown flutter slowly after him until it eventually finds the dark waters of an overflowing storm drain.

It's quickly washed out to sea with the rest of the trash.

28

PENHALLOW

I circle once above the buildings, taking one last look at the twinkling city below. The view's not so bad. I should have tried this flying thing more often.

I don't have much energy left in me, but I'm able to catch a draft and glide back to my Domain. The Nether-kin who lined the rooftops before have all scattered and disappeared—the shadows quieter than I can ever remember. It's finally stopped raining, and I see that my wards have closed their umbrellas. To my surprise, most of them still linger on the sidewalk. They're actually chatting with one another. The Hairy Man is listening to the Korean lady and politely nodding, although I'm quite certain he doesn't understand a word she says. The Pandeys smile and introduce themselves to Courtney and her practice-adult roommates. Miss Ada circulates among the firefighters, offering Halloween treats.

A quick peek at the fourth floor finds Hetty at her window. She's in her pajamas, hanging a new wind chime. The Shadow Catcher's sea glass shards twinkle blue and bright once again. I see Mamita's silhouette appear, with Tomás in her arms. She kisses Hetty on the cheek and retires to her own room without the need for any extended nighttime rituals.

Hetty places her hands on the sill, and I watch her crane her neck up toward the sky. She squints, then smiles. She can't possibly see me up here, can she? Regardless, I smile back when the room goes dark.

On this night, Hetty's not afraid to turn off her lamp.

I'm ready to sleep too. There's no telling for how long. When I wake up I'll take an inventory of my new scars—of which there are plenty. But before I rest, there's one more person I need to check on. Not a ward, but a friend.

My wings labor as I pass over my rooftop, but Viola's no longer there. I check the neighboring roofs and alleyways with no better luck. My eyelids grow heavy and I know I need to get to my perch before it's too late. But

I need to find Viola. I can't bear to have another friend leave without saying goodbye.

Finally, I spot her. She's hurrying through the streets several blocks away. I descend quickly and hit the pavement behind her with a graceless thud. There's a squeal of rubber as a yellow taxi thumps its brakes. I'm not concerned with who might see my stone form.

"Viola, wait!" I call, but she doesn't hear.

"It's me! Don't go!" I try to take flight again, but my wings barely lift me. Viola's moving with such urgency that something must be wrong.

I forget about my Domain and my perch and head off in pursuit. Now that Viola's no longer pretending to be human, she's as quick as a Netherkin and never once pauses to look back.

I beat my wings for as long as I'm able, gliding just above the ground between long strides. But soon my wings lie useless across my back and my heavy footfalls thump against the yellow lines on the pavement.

Fatigue clouds my senses. I lose track of time. Viola always remains just at the farthest edge of my vision, but before I know it, the glow of the city is far behind me. The road has turned narrow and tree-lined. The Colonial houses all have yards and gardens and split-rail fences, some of the homes mounted with wooden placards that announce construction dates older than my own. Up ahead, two headlights cut through the darkness. I summon my strength and make it into the brush alongside the road before the newspaper delivery truck rumbles past. It eventually disappears the way I came and I'm alone again in this predawn hour. I squint ahead.

I've lost Viola.

The weight of my body is becoming unbearable. Fallen leaves crackle and branches snap as I trip through the woods. Inside houses, dogs awaken and howl in alarm.

Viola, where are you? I can't chase you any farther.

I'm about to collapse when I spot a low stone wall nestled under a canopy of bare maples. A rusted iron gate is cracked open between two granite pillars. Beyond it, a tiny cemetery beckons.

It will have to do.

I stumble through the gate and find myself surrounded by a dozen thin gray headstones. It's peaceful here. Familiar, even. There are no Netherkin, and yet I don't feel alone. The ground is lined with a thick bed of fallen leaves. They look so soft and inviting.

When I fall, they cushion the blow.

I lie there for a long while. My thoughts come slowly. When they do arrive, they're fuzzy and hard to grasp.

Look at that. The sun is just starting to peek up over

the horizon. This is the first time it's cracked the clouds in a week. The light reflects off the ground, and I see that my bed of leaves is a brilliant crimson.

Dawn arrives with a head of steam, as if making up for lost days. Through its bright glow I see that someone else has joined me in the cemetery. It's a girl. She wears a woolen newsboy cap and a threadbare pea coat that's no longer smoldering. Her hands are tucked into its pockets. I'm relieved to see that she again looks the way I remembered her.

Viola stops when she reaches me and takes a knee by my side.

"Hello, Goyle," she says.

"Please don't call me Goyle," I say sleepily, and curl my stone lip into a smirk. "The name's Penhallow."

"I know," she says, and returns my smile. Her face is porcelain in the morning light. She points to something over me.

It's a headstone.

The engraved words are shallow and faded but still legible.

PENHALLOW FITCH
1875–1887

"This was me?" I ask.

"Long ago. Penhallow Fitch was a farmer's son, the youngest of six siblings. He came down with consumption—that's what they used to call tuberculosis back then. They didn't have vaccines or medications."

My voice is fading. "What do you know about him—or is it me? The boy, Penhallow?"

"Not much, except what I was able to read in the old journals. Penhallow was described as a kind boy. Curious. Well-read. He had a sarcastic sense of humor." She raises a knowing eyebrow. "But was always in good spirits. He was very brave, right up until the end."

Viola reaches down and her bare fingers touch my cold wing.

"He was also very much loved . . . by his father especially. Cyrus Fitch also had a passion for music. He shared his talent with his ailing son whenever he could take a break from the fields. He'd play his violin until his fingers ached, often deep into the night, long after Penhallow fell asleep."

I already know this story, even as Viola shares it for the first time. It was the vivid image I saw and felt when I touched the violin string.

"Where's your violin case?" I ask.

"It was never really mine to begin with. The string

inside it came from Cyrus's violin. It's *your* Remnant—
and it's now yours to do with as you wish."

I blink slowly.

"I left it with Hetty," Viola explains. "She'll hold it for
safekeeping until you're ready to claim it. I also told her
about her father's journals . . . and where to find them."

I glance around the peaceful graveyard with new eyes.
I see the name Cyrus Fitch on the headstone next to
me, Adele Fitch beside it. John, Henry, Grace, Madeline,
Quincy, and others share plots nearby—all with the same
surname. It's a family cemetery.

"You led me here on purpose," I say.

Viola pushes herself up from her crouch and offers a
shrug. "Everyone should have the opportunity to know
where they came from."

A hint of sadness crosses Viola's face, and I can only
wish she had a chance to know the same. Unfortunately, I
don't have the energy to say it.

"Thank you" is the best I can muster.

"More people than you can imagine should be thank-
ing *you*," she says.

"Just tell them to keep the pigeons off my head."

Viola flashes a little grin. "You need to rest now."

She hesitates, and rubs her thumb and forefinger along
the crimson streak in her pigtail as if she wants to say

more. But instead, she just says, "Goodbye, Penhallow," and turns to leave.

I don't have many words left in me.

"Do you have to go?" I whisper.

Viola looks back over her shoulder and replies with a gentle nod.

"Where?" I ask.

"I'm on to what's Next," she says. "You stay here. For as long as you need to. When you're ready, I'll be waiting there to meet you."

She offers a final smile, and I watch as she walks deeper into the tiny cemetery. The grounds now seem to stretch on forever, far past the boundaries of the uneven stone walls, until eventually I see Viola no more.

I blink once.

This seems like a perfect place to stay for a while.

I blink twice.

For the moment, my wards can spare me.

I blink a third time. A breeze stirs the autumn air, gentle yet strong. It scatters the leaves over my body like a crimson blanket.

Then I close my eyes.

It may be a long time before you hear from me again. But don't worry.

I'll be watching.

GOYLE-ISMS

(How to Speak Grotesque in Plain English, by Penhallow)

Bone Masons: The secret society of stone carvers once tasked with creating the world's Grotesques. Like postal workers, Bone Masons face an occupation in steep decline. But the carefully guarded secrets of the few remaining practitioners are all that defend the border between the living and the dead.

bricks: Like %##@, #@*&, and other four-letter words unsuitable for print.

Domain: Home, sweet home. The structure on which a Grotesque resides.

gargoyles: Glorified water fountains.

Grotesques: Guardians, peacekeepers, Night Wardens, and indispensable protectors of all that is good and just in the world. Okay, that last bit may be somewhat of an embellishment.

hop your perch: Stop sitting around and get off the roof. See also *shed your shell.*

imps: Troublesome minor spirits. Like flies, they buzz, bother, and occasionally bite, but they are also easily squashed with a swift swat of the tail.

Maker: The Bone Mason responsible for creating a Grotesque is referred to as his Maker. Some Makers, like mine, are gifted artists known for rendering Grotesques that are powerful *and* breathtakingly beautiful. Although, as evidenced by the Twins, even the best Makers have off days.

Netherkin: Awful, malignant spirits. The only good Netherkin is a well-digested one.

Next: As in, what comes Next? The afterlife. The great unknown that ultimately lies beyond the grave remains as mysterious to Grotesques as it does to our wards.

practice-adults: College students. Nocturnal creatures who seem to serve no useful purpose other than to keep taverns and pizza delivery people in business.

Shadow Men: The vilest of all types of Netherkin. Mysterious shapeshifters who visit sleeping children in their beds. More cunning and clever than your typical poltergeist, their specialty is theft and their prize is the most valuable treasure of all. I have a particular distaste for Shadow Men—which doesn't stop me from devouring them on sight.

shed your shell: Leave your stone body behind and travel about town as a wisp. A practice highly frowned upon by our European elders; we all do it here in the New World.

squid: A particularly odd human who can talk to the dead. Soft, fleshy, and awkward—like a squid out of water.

wards: Inhabitants of our Domains. We serve them dutifully, whether they deserve it or not. You may choose your friends, but you can't pick your wards.

wisp: The form we take when we shed our shell. A little-known fact: Grotesques can't shapeshift indiscriminately as wisps. While we can all assume the form of a human, anything else is a tricky matter. I can't change into a ferocious dragon or a woolly mammoth. Our choice of forms is limited to those creatures depicted, at least in part, by our stone shells. Sure, I'd make a rather handsome bat or vulture, but flying, well, that takes practice. And who likes practice?

AUTHOR'S NOTE

I lived and studied in Boston for seven years. I didn't have a car at the time, and like Penhallow, I roamed the streets and subways by foot. It's a very old city—at least by American standards—one where you might step out of a modern skyscraper only to pass an eighteenth-century meetinghouse. Or look down and find yourself on the historic red-bricked Freedom Trail while walking to the corner store.

I have tried to evoke that unique sense of place in *The Last Gargoyle*. Many things in the book are completely real. For example, the Granary Burying Ground, Symphony Hall, and the North End are actual locations you can and should visit. Others, like the Spite House and the hidden concert hall beneath Old Croak's, are inspired by real places but have been embellished for the sake of the story. And, of course, some things are made up entirely. Remember, I'm a novelist—an unrepentant teller of fibs—and when the facts don't fit my narrative, I'm inclined to invent new ones.

All of that said, I won't comment on whether a solitary stone Grotesque resides on a rooftop overlooking Boston's streets. And if one does, I certainly won't tell you where to find him. I don't think the building's owners would welcome you sniffing around. But I will say this: Should you stumble upon our hero, please don't mention I sent you. And whatever you do, *don't* call him Goyle.

—Paul Durham

PENHALLOW'S REAL-WORLD HAUNTS

Many of the locations and neighborhoods in *The Last Gargoyle* are real places you can visit in Boston.

- Boston Common (the "Common")
- Boston Conservatory at Berklee (the "Conservatory")
- Boylston Street Station
- Copp's Hill Burying Ground
- The Fens
- Granary Burying Ground
- North End
- Old North Church
- Prudential Center (the "glass-and-steel tower on Boylston Street")
- Symphony Hall
- Theater District